The Jamie A. Moore Story
A NOVEL

L. Diane Estes

www.ldianeestes.com

The Library of Congress Cataloging-in-Publication Data is available upon request.

February 2017

ISBN-13: 978-1542630344

ISBN-10: 1542630347

Isolation, betrayal, desperation, secrets of crime-
her perfect idea of him was a chance at a new life...

Jamie Moore lost the most important man in her life at the age of 13. She was a daddy's girl who followed her father's every move. But, she was in for a rude awakening after his death. Left with a grief-stricken mother, a sister chasing answers about her own life— loneliness slowly filled her soul.

After a few years of getting by, her mother found that man, her boyfriend. Where did he come from? Why was he now living in her daddy's home? He was not to be trusted, that man wasn't as he appeared to her mother.

In LONELINESS WITHIN author L. Diane Estes inimitably unfolds the life of Jamie the young woman as she struggles with the voice from her inner loneliness. We experience her falling deep in love with the complicated, secretive, very successful, well dressed likes of Mr. Daniel. This was all she could have wanted—needed, her dreams were coming true it appears... Beware, nothing is as it seems. Take a seat... This journey is as real as it gets!

To,

Anyone that ever felt an
unspoken internal
loneliness
or maybe developed a wall of emotional
seclusion because you felt the pressure:

to look the part...
to represent...
to role model...
to be...

Loneliness is a complicated, emotional, and unnerving reaction to separation or isolation. Feeling lonely stirs emotions inspired by a scarcity of interpersonal interaction with others on a human level. Loneliness can be experienced while accompanied by others in either a private or public setting.

Loneliness Within

The Jamie A. Moore Story
A NOVEL

L. Diane Estes

Prologue

I was a teenager when tragedy struck our home. My family had never dealt with such pain and grief, at least not to this extent before that horrible ordeal. Nothing would have ever prepared me for the separation and emptiness of losing him. It's more than I can explain with words. I didn't know how to stop it from consuming me at the time. We were all in for a rude awakening, sooner rather than later.

My parents, James and Diana, were high school friends who reunited through a mutual friend years later. They dated, fell in love, and got married—almost like a fairytale. My older sister, Kelsie, and I grew up surrounded by love. She would tease me, "Oh Jamie, stop being so serious!" She was always more outgoing and personable than I am; people call me an "old soul." I've always been a deep thinker, to myself, but able to talk to just about anyone, old or young.

Daddy used to say, "The best things in life are nothing without your family to share them with." Our parents were never afraid of showing us they loved us. My dad was a true family man. He cared about us and always made sure we knew we were important, that we knew we were taken care of, supported. He made sure we went to church and were thankful of what we had. My dad was a hardworking man. He took care of us because it was the right thing to do. He liked to spend weekends fixing his 1970 Chevrolet truck—he called "The Longhorn". There was always something wrong with it. He enjoyed teaching Kelsie and me about every single greasy part under the hood. But, more than that, he always wanted us around him. He wanted us to spend quality time together. It meant a lot to him to have us listen, and he loved it when little old me would ask a hundred questions over and over.

I was a daddy's girl. I'd follow him to the ends of the earth, Mama too. There is no place on earth I wouldn't follow my parents. They're everything in the world to me. But Kelsie? Well, she was the reason I looked so pretty all the time. She did everything for me, and I followed her too when I could. I never liked being left behind. If Daddy's truck was moving, I was in it. There was so much of the world to explore, so many things I wanted to see and learn.

The Saturday mornings Daddy was off work were the best. We had breakfast first, cleaning second, and then we played hide-and-seek as a family. No one could ever find Daddy—he knew all the best hiding places. I'm the one who was caught all the time. When I could hear their breathing, I'd burst out laughing, completely unable to contain myself. These were good times.

My mama was the most beautiful woman in the world. She had a natural beauty that shone through. She'd straighten her long hair until it was as fine as silk. She had a slender waist and didn't have to do much to keep it that way. She dressed simply during the week and like *Lady Di* on the weekends. Her voice was unique, subtle but forceful. We knew when she meant business. She was average height for a woman. Her soft skin was passed down to Kelsie and me. My mama wasn't much of a talker, but she acted like she didn't realize it. She spent most of her days making handcrafted quilts. She made them in different sizes and sold them to the church, neighbors, and anyone else who wanted one. She liked to embroider and bake too. It was one way she helped with the household finances. I never could understand how she was able to sit and focus on those quilts for hours on end, just sitting at that old, white, battered machine. Her sewing machine was important to her. It really meant something; she refused to get a new one. Sometimes when it didn't work, she would sew by hand until her fingers ached. She'd rest a while and then go right back to sewing. It gave her purpose and made her happy, I guess.

And me? I was everywhere at once. My mind raced, and I was much too busy for my own good. I couldn't sit still for much of anything. Between dancing ballet with Kelsie, dressing up, and writing in my notebooks on the back porch, I kept myself busy. I like to write my thoughts down, but I love composing poems—even if they're about things only I would care about. I didn't have very many friends, which some people said was sad, but I never thought so. With all the love, I had from my family, I didn't miss it. I was too deep of a thinker for kids my age to understand.

Kelsie was a dreamer. Life for her always seemed unsettled, but she encouraged me to be the best I could, to follow my passion. She fussed at me too. She'd say things like, "Jamie, hold your arms down at your side, stand up, back straight, and walk with grace." I told her so many times that we could only imitate the ladies on TV who walked the runways. We never trained like they did and I wasn't getting paid to walk like them. She would laugh at my little rant. I didn't know what I'd do without her.

Chapter One

1984

My parents were very private about their personal stuff; they shielded us from everything. We seemed to have some problems, though—mostly with money. It happened from time to time, I'm sure of it, but I don't have any details. I tried to listen in on my parent's conversations, but the thin bedroom walls muffle their voices and I couldn't make out what they were saying, not clearly at least. I wanted to know more than I should have, but that's just how I am. I always want to know more.

Even though we have just enough to get by, we are admired in our neighborhood. All the other women on our street envied my mother. If I paid close attention, I could sometimes hear them mumbling under their breath, "That Diana sure got herself a good man." They envied her from a distance, but wouldn't dare speak those words to her face. It almost seemed like a compliment. The women around here tended to gossip and would rather have been quietly envious than tell a person to their face how good they've got it.

Ms. Maple across the street was the most interesting neighbor we had. She had two husbands and now a "situation," at least that's the word on the street. Let's see, first it was Mr. Jeffery, then Mr. Alexander, and finally the man she's with now, Mr. Arthur Lee Preston. Folks said she was crazier than crazy and got a government check for it too. I saw her go off on Mr. Alexander in the yard one night, hitting him in the head with a broom handle. I was so scared for him. They said she ran all those men away, everyone except Mr. Preston. He got a monthly check too from being in the military, and she ain't about to run that off. Besides, he was a little crazy too. He fought in the Vietnam War and it got to him. That happened a lot around here. The men go to war and leave as one person before coming back someone else. It's mighty strange and I'm glad Daddy didn't do that. Seeing all that death and having a hand in it, maybe it's just too much for them to handle. I never wanted to be mean like that—the kind of person who was never happy with any one. I will marry a man just like my daddy. Our pastor said women shouldn't be dominant and feisty like Ms. Maple.

We walked to church on Sunday mornings, and sometimes to the park after dinner. We weren't like most families around here. A lot of them didn't have fathers, and those that do, well, most don't take their kids to church. Daddy said maybe if he led by example, some of the other men would feel pressured to follow, which makes me laugh. I wanted to tell him I don't think they're following much of anything. Everyone does their own thing around these parts. Daddy knows all the secrets of our neighborhood, but neither he nor Mama ever speaks of them.

Most of Daddy's friends came to our house for advice because they said he was a great friend and listener. He always had a Bible scripture ready to help anyone who needed it, no matter what their problems were. He had a way with people, a presence that made them trust and listen to him. But there were some friends he never heard from again, like Mr. Jackson.

Mr. Jackson played the guitar in a band called Arista Moon. The streets were always calling his name. He told Daddy he felt suffocated and miserable being a family man. He had a wife and three kids, but never kept a regular job. He was afraid of hard work, even his hands didn't look like a man's should. They were soft, like a lady's—Mr. Jackson never did any hard work. The band was a little popular on the local circuit, but they never recorded an album.

His wife would call Mama crying at night, asking for help. Mr. Jackson wouldn't stop running after his dreams so he could give them what they needed. My dad finally sat him down one day, while I was sitting behind them pretending to play with the wheels on my skates.

He said firmly, "Jackson, you have to decide what's more important to you: living your dreams or feeding those babies you have at home. You have left that woman more than five times now. When it don't work out on the streets, you come running back home hoping Helen will take you back. That woman needs help. She's doing the best she can, but you need to take some time and decide what you think God would want you to do."

I went on playing after Mr. Jackson walked off and I don't recall ever seeing him again, at least not at our house. His wife, Ms. Helen, and her children, well, they moved to Georgia to live with her elderly grandmother. Mama said, "It was plain ole' sad. Makes you rejoice you have someone who don't mind being a family man."

My father spent a lot of time telling to us about God. He taught us what we should be like as young women—how we should respect ourselves and that we're special gifts from God. He said to keep our minds on school, to focus on going to college and making a good life. He taught us to put our family and ourselves first.

My daddy made everything in our home run well, but he worked too much. He refused to work on Sunday, which he called "the Lord's Day." He told us Sundays belong to the family, but, most importantly, it is a day for us to have fellowship with God. We could give all the other days to the world, but Sunday's we put God first. One Sunday, when we were walking, my daddy noticed a man lying on the bus stop bench. Daddy stopped, gave him a few dollars.

"Sir, my name is James and my church is within walking distance from here. I'd like to invite you to church with me."

The man took the money quickly out of Daddy's hand and replied, "Naw, not this time, man. Maybe next time." He picked up his blanket and backpack and walked off without ever looking back.

Chapter Two

1986

    The breeze stood still that morning, allowing the heat to sit and sink in. I didn't hear the birds chirping; it was quiet, just the hum of the air conditioner by the bushes. The back porch needed sweeping, dust and debris from the yard was everywhere. It always was after a windy or rainy day. But if I volunteered to sweep, Mama would have asked me to sweep every day I was out there. I decided to pass on that and just dust it off enough to sit down. I wondered where the sun was; it was so hot, but rather cloudy and humid. I could feel that summer sun, but couldn't see it. A glimpse caught my eye; I saw a yellow glow hiding behind the clouds, occasionally peeking out. Well good, I thought, At least my skin won't burn off today. I love the summer—we've been out for a few weeks now—no school, no worries. I could sit and write in my notebooks as long as I wanted. Writing is soothing and it helps me pass the time. I'm not much of a late sleeper, so I'm generally up with the birds. I decided to get out of the heat and head inside a little earlier than usual.

The television was always on; we only had one in the house. It sat on the living room floor, taking up so much space. The news said the Astros had signed a new player, Eric Anthony. I didn't think I could ever sit still long enough to watch a baseball game—they're too slow for me. I had been flipping channels earlier and there wasn't anything on but reruns. I was bored and desperate to get out of the house that day. There were so many things I wanted to do, but I thought I'd wait for Daddy to get home, maybe I'd ask him to take me to the store. I wanted Kelsie to fix my hair too, so it can last. If I was going out of this house with Daddy today, I needed to look decent, but I also needed someone else in order to do it all. Kelsie always slept in so late, making it hard to get anything done in the morning. It was the middle of the week; she didn't have anything else to do but sleep. I should've told Mama she was still seeing that boy. Mama told her he wasn't any good, but her head is as hard as a brick. You couldn't tell her anything. Kelsie needed to figure everything out the hard way. I sure wished she'd listened to Daddy more and loved God like he said we should. I love God because I'm supposed to—it's that simple.

The phone had been ringing non-stop. I wondered if Mama couldn't hear it or if she was ignoring it while she cooked. I wandered back inside and headed to the kitchen; I decided to answer it and save Mama the trouble.

"Hello, this is the Moore residence."

"Hi miss, this is Joe from James's work. Can I speak with Mrs. Moore, please? It's an emergency."

"Hold on." I put the phone down. "Mama, Joe is on the phone from Daddy's job." Mama turned the burner off and picked up the receiver. I left the kitchen as she answered.

"Yes? Hello, this is Diana. What? He's where?"

Mama's voice seemed worried, but I heard Kelsie thump out of bed and stumble into the bathroom. I walked down the hall and into her room. She came back from the bathroom still in her pajamas.

"Kelsie, you finally woke up."

"Jamie, do you hear that?"

"What?"

"Hush. Listen. Is that Mama? Is she crying?"

"Let's go see." I led Kelsie to the kitchen where Mama sat at the table, breakfast still half-finished, and the phone still in her hands. "Mama, are you okay?" I asked quietly.

I could feel the world shift as everything around me changed. I wasn't inside my body anymore; I watched my life unfold from a distance and I couldn't snap out of it. Mama dropped the phone, ran out the front door, and down the street barefoot. I saw it happen in slow motion. Kelsie stood dumbfounded for a moment, before we chased after her, calling out to her, afraid of dashing after her with our own bare feet.

"Mama! Mama, what happened?" I yelled.

She never looked back, never said a word. Why wouldn't she answer us? She headed straight for Ms. Marie's front door. She's the only person who lived nearby that we could rely on while Daddy was at work. She had a car and she was such a nice lady. Tears filled my eyes, overflowing down my cheeks and dripping onto my shoulders and down my shirt. I couldn't see clearly and I couldn't stop them. Mama beat on Ms. Marie's door, rattling the screen on its hinges.

Kelsie was crying and asking, "Mama, are you okay? What happened?"

All I could do was stand in shock; speechless, knowing it had something to do with Daddy.

Before Ms. Marie could get the door open, Mama screamed, "Its James! Something's wrong. He was rushed to the hospital from work. Can you please drop me and the kids off at the hospital?"

Ms. Marie agreed without hesitation and went back inside to grab her purse and keys. Mama asked her to pick us up at our house, so we could get our things together too. Kelsie kept repeating her questions until Mama finally turned and looked at us.

She gathered herself together for a moment and said, "I don't know. Go in the house get your shoes I need to change close and grab my purse. Make sure the back door is locked and then come right out."

It was the longest ride I've ever taken even though it was just ten minutes. Mama scared us so badly. She was frantic like never before. This couldn't be real. They must have made a mistake, I knew my daddy was fine—he had to be.

"Mama, Daddy's going to be okay. Don't worry," I said, knowing she must have felt something awful inside her heart to make her so sad. Daddy was going to be okay, I kept telling myself. All he needed was a little rest in the hospital. I promise I won't bother you anymore when you come home, Daddy. I won't ask you any more silly questions.

Our entire world changed that day. The world rushed back into focus. I was slammed back into my body. I wasn't in a dream even though it seemed that way; this was reality. My insides crumbled into broken pieces. When we reached the hospital floor where Daddy was, they took us to a separate area right outside his room.

It was so cold and quiet, you could hear a pin drop. We waited an eternity for someone to tell us what was going on. Then two doctors came in looking tired. They told us my father had died before he reached the hospital. His heart stopped. They tried to get it restarted, but he wasn't getting enough oxygen to his brain and his brain had failed too. The doctors were convinced there was nothing they could have done at that point. Mama and Kelsie went to Daddy's room where his lifeless body lay.

I refused to go. I looked through the window instead. I stared at his still body lying in the bed. How could I live knowing I'd never see him laugh or breathe again? His heart just couldn't handle the long hours or the stress of trying to make ends meet.

Daddy worked himself to death. He worked and loved so hard his heart stopped. How could this have happened? My safe reality died with my daddy.

Who will protect us now? How will we survive this? I called out to God to help us.

Loneliness Within

Even if it Means

A young girl without her father
Taught to survive through life's experiences
From the dark hole deep within, learning and living
Trained to tolerate and suppress the pain
She found a way to escape the rain
Her alternate route is from the starting place called a lonely heart
Her journey to locate the fuel that energizes her soul, she seeks
needed love
Love from a stranger, love from a friend, love from a man
Temporary, part time, in the meantime, either one will do
Afraid of the loneliness…scared to live without a home
A man that is…
A young girl turned into a young woman
Learned to survive like she seen the others do
The idea of dying without ever finding a soul mate
Causes her to settle for any date that comes her way
Even if it means settling for what he will give
Even if it means she has to share him and wait to live
Even if it means allowing herself to be downgraded,
Reaching an all-time low and accommodating it
A young girl that turned into a woman lingers there
That's her rescue from that alternate route with the starting place
called a lonely heart
She won't stop because she learned to do whatever it takes to
keep him
Even if it means dying ten times over again on the inside
Becoming that faded photo that was uniquely captured as a clear
image of young,
but older girl who turned into a woman on accident.

Chapter Three

1988

Everything after Daddy died is a blur. When I wake up, I think everything's normal—Daddy's just out working. Then, it hits me all at once. Suddenly, the emptiness of his absence rushes in. He's in heaven, for sure. Sometimes I feel as if he has sent me an angel, who knows? It sure would be nice to really believe that.

We've been struggling a lot the past few months, more than we ever had before. Mama spent all the money she got from Daddy's compensation and the donations from church on bills. She and Kelsie are both working hard at the market, but it's hard to keep up. I can see the stress in the bags under her eyes.

Mama isn't the same. She talks some, but not much, not that she ever did. I know she loves us, but she's stuck deep within her shell. I help out around the house as much as possible. I cook a little, but mostly I clean. I want to help bring in some money, but I can't—Mama said not right now. Mama said she didn't want me working, that it would interfere with school and all. She thinks I'm so smart and says I can be anything I want to be in life. I understand that, but right now we need the help.

I think Mama might be turning into Grandma. Grandma died alone in her home. She shut off everyone who meant anything to her, especially Mama. She was sick and was too stubborn to go to the doctor to see about her health. I know she wanted a relationship with Mama, but they shared too many bad memories, so it was better they stayed apart. Mama never talked about what happened to them, but I know Grandma dying before they could solve their problems weighs heavy on her too. First, Grandma died, and then Daddy did. Mama's in a really bad place. I catch her wandering off, gazing out the window like she's waiting for Daddy to come home.

When she isn't working, she sleeps her life away. I worry when Mama falls into too deep a sleep. I help her by wiping her face with a wet cloth, bringing her water, washing her clothes, changing her quilt out to make sure her things are clean. She becomes my baby when she's like that. I feel responsible for her. I wish she would talk to Pastor Andrews and get some help, but she won't. I know she's in the desert, dying of thirst with no way of getting water.

May God have mercy on her soul.

I need her. I need my mother. I want to talk about my life and the pains I have, but I can't. I have to deal with them myself and care for her. Kelsie helps as much as she can, but she's grown now and ready to take the first plane out of Texas. Her boyfriend left for college. They didn't really love each other—I think it was something for her to do. She's moved on from him and is dating someone else now. I think Kelsie is borrowing space here, just like me.

We used to love this old neighborhood, we felt so connected to it, but it seems foreign now. We don't go outside or take walks anymore. The light on our front porch has dimmed. The neighbors pretend we don't exist. They're afraid we may need their help, I guess—everyone except Ms. Marie. No one rings our doorbell anymore. But something still tugs at me letting me know it won't be like this forever.

Maybe it would be different if I had real friends, but I don't. I don't fit in with my classmates. The nerds I don't understand and the fast-tail girls I feel sorry for. So, I go on. I treat everyone the same—nice and polite, a little distant—and keep moving forward. My sister is the only friend I need.

∞∞∞∞

November 1988

Winter's almost here again. Mama has started getting up more when she's not working and the store loves her more than ever. They've finally agreed to let her sell her quilts; now we can earn some extra money. She's coming alive again. I can see it!

Mama's voice drifts into my room. "Jamie, come in here, please."

"Yes, Mama?"

"Come in. Sit with me here. I want to talk to you."

I walk in and sit down on the bed next to her. "I realize Kelsie's leaving soon and she may never come back."

"Yes, ma'am, but why do you say that?"

"There are a lot of things you don't know about me, your grandmother, or Kelsie. Your grandmother really hated me, I believe."

"No Mama, I don't think Grandma hated you at all. She was always sweet to everyone. She just had a different way of loving you, Mama."

"Jamie, you've always known how to rationalize things. You give everyone the benefit of the doubt. You better stop always looking for the good in everyone; folks will hurt you, Jamie. I use to be just like you. I hate to say it, but you're going to get your heart broken being like that."

"Mama, not everyone is bad. Are you okay? Is there something wrong, Mama?"

"Child, give me your hand. Don't worry. I just want to talk. Is that okay?"

Her hand feels warm, soft, and dry against mine. She squeezes it tightly.

"Yes, ma'am. I'm listening."

"Jamie, when I was younger, your grandma worked for a well to do family, the Perrys. They were one of the wealthiest families in Sugar Land. I would go to work with Grandma some days when school was out during the summers. I'd help clean and tend the younger children.

"Sometimes, they would send for me on weekends in one of their big fine fancy cars while Mr. and Mrs. Perry went out to dinner. I'd make a little extra money babysitting the little ones. They had two little girls and one older son about my age. Their home was so nice. It was bigger than our entire church. It had six bedrooms and four huge bathrooms. One room was bigger than all our rooms put together. I remember the balcony on the top floor and the porch in the backyard with nice wide steps. Oh, that kitchen was huge. It was a beautiful place fit for a king. I was proud to be there."

"Did it have a pool?" I ask quietly, but excited. Mama didn't regularly share stories.

"Yes, of course. A big pool with a hot tub too—I used to call it a 'hot pool.' I loved that house. I would tend to little Katherine and Rosemary; they loved playing with me. I taught them a lot of things, like how to hopscotch and tie their shoes, and drink milk and eat a cookie at the same time without choking. Those kids loved my mama too. They would call her 'Mama' just like I did."

"Really? Grandma had other people calling her mama? Was that strange?"

"No, honey. It was real nice actually. They liked your grandma a lot; she took care of them." Mama sighs and begins again.

"Their son's name was Benjamin, but everyone called him Ben. He was their pride and joy. They gave him whatever he wanted and protected him from everything, but they were strict with him about school. They gave him a lot of freedom, but they expected him to do well in school because he was very smart. He was handsome too—tall, eyes like a cat, and very athletic. He could swim like a fish and golf like a pro. At least, that's what I would overhear his parents saying to their friends. Ben was nice and very sweet; he was my best friend. I must be honest: he was more than my friend, Jamie. He was the love of my life."

"When my daddy died, I was young. I felt alone and scared all the time. I know how you feel, Jamie. It was like an emptiness I couldn't replace...well, not until Ben. He would talk to me. I was smart too, you know, but better at making things with my hands. I didn't like reading much, but I did it just to keep up with him as much as I could."

"So, that's why you're so smart, Mama." I grin up at her, always impressed by how much she knows about the world. She's a quiet woman; I think that makes people underestimate her.

"Yes, because most of the time, he was teaching me. They didn't teach the same stuff in the school I went to back in the neighborhood. No one ever would have suspected we were in love. He wouldn't have dared to be with a poor girl like me. Not even his mother had a clue we were that close. She felt it was nice and sweet of him to take the time to help me—that tutoring me was his way of giving back to the less fortunate; I was just something else for her to brag about." Mama looks down at her hands, folded in her lap, caught up in the memories. A sad smile crosses her face.

"Kind of like a charity case?" I ask as I worry my nail between my teeth. Mama frowns and shoos my hand out of my mouth. "But Mr. Ben didn't think of you that way, did he?"

"No, of course not. He was fair and he didn't see a difference between us. He'd bring me diagrams, books, and articles to read. He also bought me fabric and my very first sewing machine. He bought me a real nice one for my birthday. I still have it."

I stop fidgeting and look up, surprised. "Mama, is it the old white one you still use?"

She smiles and for just a moment, I can see the happy young girl she had been. "Yes, it is. I promised him I would keep it always. I made him a pillow and he kept it for as long as I could remember. He would talk about life, scientific theories, and the body's anatomy. I wanted to learn more. He was so passionate about making sure I learned as much as I could. Jamie, you're old enough for me to talk to you straight. I loved that man more than I have ever loved anyone and he knew it. I believed he loved me just as much. It didn't matter what color my skin was, or how poor my family was—he loved me for me. I could tell. It was the way he touched me and looked into my eyes. He would sneak kisses and hug me every chance he could. We couldn't stand being apart, even just for a day or two."

"You kissed him? I can't picture you kissing anyone but Daddy."

"I didn't know your daddy then."

"I know, but it still makes me feel funny thinking about all of this. You and Daddy were perfect together. He loved you—us—to the ends of the earth."

"That he did. Ben loved me too, but it was young love. One day he decided to play doctor with me. I was about your age, sixteen, and he was seventeen and a senior year in high school. He said he wanted to examine me for a science project. He asked me to get completely undressed and lie down on his bed. Well, I did it. I trusted him with everything I had in me. I would have jumped over fire for him. He began to examine me, but it wasn't like a doctor would a patient, more like a husband would his wife. His hands were soft and shaky, nervous-like. I asked him what exactly was he doing. He looked at me and told me I had the smoothest, softest, brown skin he had ever seen in his life. And he knew in his heart he loved me, so he kissed me, and I kissed him back. The rest just happened unlike anything I had ever known at the time. Neither of us had experience doing what we did, but it didn't matter at the time. Later, he said he didn't want any other girls. He asked me to go to college with him. He didn't want to leave without me. He said we would be together forever. I told him he was the only man on earth I would ever love."

"But you didn't love only him. You loved Daddy too."

"I did love your father, very much, still do, even though he's with the Lord now. But Ben was my first love and first loves are special."

"I don't know if I want to fall in love." I say, but Mama just shakes her head at me.

"Ben and I, we kept our love a secret for a long time. We had so much time together alone. His parents would never have understood him loving me, and my mama wouldn't have either. If they found out, they would've fired her on the spot and I would never have seen him again. We weren't going to risk it. I didn't want to be without him, so we kept it quiet. It was our secret until..."

"What happened?" I ask, leaning forward intently.

"I remember being sick and feeling so tired. I threw up at least three times the day before. I remember thinking that I hadn't had my woman time visit me at all that month or the month before. Mama would say stress

21

could mess with your monthly at times. I was worried sick about him leaving for college, so surely that was what was affecting me. I will never forget the night before I left to go home. I pulled Ben into his dad's study and told him I didn't get my cycle and that I'd been feeling really sick. He looked at me and asked me what I was trying to tell him, but he already knew.

"I looked straight into his eyes and said, 'Benjamin Perry III, I might be pregnant and I'm scared. What are we going to do?'"

He was ready to go and tell his parents. We couldn't believe what was happening. He looked sad and terrified at the same time. I felt bad, not for me, but for him. His parents would kill him and surely fire Mama. I asked him not to tell them because I knew it would be devastating. Mama would kill me; plus, he had to leave for school. I told him I would deal with it. He disagreed. He wasn't okay with me going through it alone. I wondered how could I stop him from going to college—how could I be the one to hold up his future? He had a scholarship a whole life ahead of him. I wouldn't be responsible for ruining that. He told me we would talk about it more the next time I came to visit him. I begged him again not to say a word to his parents. As we stepped out of the study, Ben stopped me in the doorway and kissed me. I had the undeniable feeling that someone was watching. When I pulled back, I caught sight of Mama out of the corner of my eye. She was standing in the hall watching us kiss. The look on her face told me she was not pleased. Our secret was out. In the thick of it all, with anger blazing in her eyes, she said I would never return to the Perry's' home again. And I didn't."

"But, Mama, you were pregnant. Why didn't they let you see him?"

"I'm getting there—be patient. I stayed at home pregnant, alone, and scared out of mind with a broken heart. Ben begged to see me; I know he did. I would sneak and call him whenever I could. When he tried to call back, Mama told him I was either sick or not home. She had forbidden me from going back to their house. After not being allowed to talk to me for weeks, he finally told his parents the truth. He stood strong and said that whatever they were going to do, they would just have to do it. I yearned for him and I got sicker—not just because I was pregnant, but because I knew they would never let us be together. The Perry's fired Mama shortly after he told them the truth and she never forgave me for that."

"But it was just a job, you were young—my age. Why didn't she forgive you?"

"Jobs were hard to come by and my mama was a proud woman. She didn't approve of what I'd done and didn't like that she was the one paying for it. She felt as if I betrayed her trust."

"But you were the one having a baby."

"She was the one keeping a roof over my head."

If Daddy was alive and I came home pregnant, my parents would be furious, but they wouldn't hate me. Mama would understand—she'd have to. Daddy would have been disappointed, but he was a man who believed God doesn't give us more than we can handle.

"I get it, Mama. Go on." She pats my hand.

"All communication between us was cut off and eventually he left for school. I was alone. Much later, I found out he wrote me letters, but Mama never gave me any of them. It wasn't until I overheard her talking to Aunt Mae that I found out about them. She threw them in the trash. I couldn't understand how she could do that to me. He loved me like I felt he did. She returned the checks the Perry's sent her for my baby. We were dirt poor, Jamie. Lord knows we needed every dime to help take care of your sister, but my mama was a proud woman."

"What happened to my sister?"

"Well, she grew up with you baby."

"Kelsie?"

"She was the most beautiful, pale, bright-eyed baby I've ever seen."

"Daddy wasn't her father?"

"No, her father is Dr. Benjamin Alexander Perry III—the man who took my heart to California with him when he left for college. Kelsie looks like him—her eye color, her dimples are just like his. Sometimes, I can't stand to look at her because she reminds me too much of him. I thought he was a mistake. I was angry for so long until I found out the truth."

"What truth?"

"Mama was cold towards me after that happened and our relationship never recovered. She blamed me for everything. She made me feel like I was a slut, though she never said it directly. I was so glad to get out of that house. But the odd thing is she was so proud to show off Kelsie to her friends. She would even say tell Kelsie how much she looked like her father right in front of James. It made my skin crawl and she knew it. I thought for sure she was doing it to hurt me. I remember seeing Rosemary, the youngest Perry girl, at the Christmas Wish Charity event some years ago. Your sister was 10 and they looked exactly alike, her and Rosemary—they have the same eyes and nose. Rosemary looked at your sister and smiled before looking at me. She hugged me tight, but never said a word. I was volunteering in street clothes, unlike them, and I was too ashamed to say anything."

"She could have said something, Mama. Why didn't she tell you where to find Mr. Ben?"

"Well, from what I knew at the time, he had a medical practice in California and was living well. If he didn't think enough of me to find me, or Kelsie, after all those years, then my words to his sister wouldn't have meant anything. I was like my mama, a prideful woman; at that point in my life, I didn't want his handouts. I was with your father and he was a good man. I did, however, want him to acknowledge her and get to know our daughter. But, that was a dream. Ben eventually got married and had other children."

"But he never wanted to know Kelsie? She kind of doesn't have a daddy." Mama's face goes stern and she looked me dead in the eye.

"Honey, your father loved Kelsie like she was his own and he claimed her as such. Don't you ever say she didn't have a father. The only difference was she was here before we got married, that's all. He was a good man, a great father—someone she could be proud to call 'Daddy.' I believe things happen the way they're supposed to. My mama just didn't respect the love and connection I had with Ben. We meant more to each other than just a roll in the hay. He talked to me about his thoughts and feelings, the pressure his parents placed on him, and how he was always afraid of disappointing them. He couldn't be himself around them."

"Mama, does this still bother you?"

"Yes, sometimes it does. I think from time to time about the 'what-ifs.' I wonder what could have been and it bothers me. Losing your dad brings back that emptiness and loneliness. I don't like talking about it because it's too painful for me."

Mama takes a deep breath and steadies her nerves while I sit quietly for a moment.

"Jamie, I told your sister the truth some time ago and she hasn't been the same since. She's been chasing Ben's footsteps since that day. She's determined to get to California to meet him. I begged her not to tell you any of this. She's struggling and trying to fill the hole left by your daddy's death. Knowing the truth about her father didn't make her problems any better. She needs some help—she wants to feel complete. I'm not certain finding him is the answer, but only she'll know. I can't sit back and watch her get her heart broken if he rejects her, but there's nothing I can do to change her mind."

I pull Mama close and hug her tightly. Today was a great start for her. She opened up to me more than she ever has before. She obviously needed to talk her feelings out and I think it might've helped. I'm scared though; nothing I thought about my family is true except that we grew up loved. I had no idea so many hidden secrets were prowling around the corner. Why do families around here have so many secrets? If you don't ask then no one tells anything. What else is hiding in the dark? After that story about her and Kelsie's real father, I wonder if Daddy isn't my father either. Is Mama just waiting on the right time to tell me too?

Chapter Four

April 1989

Summer lurks around the corner again and graduation is rapidly approaching. Kelsie and I talk every day about life and her leaving town. She's still my best friend, but I'll lose that when she's gone. I know things will change once she leaves. I'll miss her being here at the house. What happens when I need to talk—we can't afford long distance calls? I don't like that she's leaving. I'm not good with people leaving me.

As for me, I managed not to get pregnant, drop out of school, or run away with a no-good boy—which isn't much of an accomplishment. High school boys just aren't for me. They say I'm stuck up and that I think I'm better than them. They don't understand I'm just not willing to put out like the other girls. I remember what Daddy used to say, "You're special and smart. You are who God made you—an amazing person." Anytime I thought about getting a boyfriend, I'd think back to that. I'm still maturing. I have time.

Loneliness Within

Mama is a little better these days, but not completely herself. I think she's trying to occupy her time by spending a lot of hours working, far more than usual. What will happen if she never finds her way back to how she was before Daddy died? What if all the tragedy and loneliness she felt over the years overtake her mind forever? I can't think like that now. I'll be her sole provider when Kelsie leaves. I have to think positively.

Kelsie stopped going to school this semester so she could work full time to help Mama with the bills. She's also saving money so she can be on her own. Mama knew she couldn't stop Kelsie from leaving, so she told her to always have money put aside to make a phone call home and enough to get back just in case of an emergency. Kelsie really wants to know her father; she won't rest until she's met him. I don't understand—Daddy's the one who raised her. Her own father never knew her. Maybe I'll understand one day, but right now, I want to scream. She's so stubborn.

Kelsie always teased me about dressing better, and the older I get, the more I agree with her. I need to dress more like an adult. She thinks I'm the most beautiful person she's ever seen—on TV or anywhere. She says I hide my beauty because I haven't embraced it. I just don't think I'm as pretty as she is. Everyone, all our schoolmates, the neighbors, and even the church members agree with me. Well, they never say it, but I can see it in their eyes. I'm not sure if it's her fair complexion or her eye color being so different and all.

She resembles Mama a little, but she must look just like her father. She keeps saying she wants me to take better care of myself and not wait around for her to do my hair. She's been looking after my hair since I was little and Mama taught her how. She had to be taught—her hair is so different. I have the long, unmanageable, course hair and she has Barbie doll straight, fine hair. I always thought it was unfair that she got such different genes than I did from our parents, but it all makes sense now. Either way, if she's leaving I need to learn how to take care of my own wild hair and how to dress.

I want to be just like her in so many ways. And now she's teaching me how to put on makeup, even though I'll never wear it in public. I look so different when I'm dressed up. I've always been plain and happy being so, but dressing up makes me feel special, like a model or actress. Kelsie makes me take pictures and walk around the house like it's a runway. I shouldn't cry about this anymore, but I'll miss her so much after she's gone.

Today I noticed Kelsie watching me. I guess she's noticed I've taken more time working on myself. She said she was proud of me. I can't understand why am I so afraid to wear things that showoff my body a little? Probably because I'm only skin and bones. But, I remember Daddy's words: "God made you just the way you are for a reason."

Kelsie's always saying that unlike her, I don't have to wear makeup to be pretty. She thinks I'm naturally beautiful, which is more than anyone can ask a sister to say. So, I'm trying to stop thinking of myself in a negative way. I don't have to be like other people—I can focus on being the best me. I wish I believed it. I do hide behind my clothes, my ponytail, and the books I read. I'm trying to learn that I can display my beauty and be smart at the same time. Kelsie keeps saying I think too much. While I don't agree with her, I really should stop worrying and live more. I lie in bed with my back against my pillows and stare at the ceiling, thinking what I can do to live more and worry less. I chuckle at my own thoughts—I'm worrying about worrying.

Kelsie's door creaks open and she hollers, "Jamie! Come here for a minute, please? There's something I want to tell you."

"What is it?" I haul myself out of bed and trudge down the hallway before letting myself into Kelsie's room.

Clothes are scattered everywhere, her bed's unmade, and I see two—no, four—water glasses. I pull out her desk chair to sit down, only to find a pile of books and folded up travel maps.

"You need to clean up this room, Kelsie. There's nowhere to sit.

"Sit down here on the floor with me. I need help polishing my toes.

"Kelsie, you know I hate painting your toes. The smell of the nail polish always gives me a headache." Kelsie sighs heavily. She quickly stands and walks over to the window, heaving it open.

"There, now it won't give you a headache. But I need to tell you something and it's a good distraction."

"You need to know, so I'm telling you that Mama has a man friend."

"She met a man?"

"What? I had no idea Mama wanted to date."

"Jamie, he comes by the store sometimes and they've started dating."

"What? Dating like going out as a couple or just as friends?" I can't wrap my head around my mother being with anyone but Daddy. The oily feeling of betrayal runs through me.

"I guess they're more than friends now. This has been going on for months."

"Kels, how could Mama do this to Daddy? How could she treat him like that?"

First, she's still in love with Kelsie's father and now she's up and on to a new man. What happened to loving someone is forever? Isn't that what people vow when they marry? I guess I don't know Mama like I thought I did. Maybe I'm just not ready to see her with another man, especially since she's still a little fragile. I want her to be happy, I do. It's just so surprising that she wouldn't tell me this herself. I know I'm protective of her.

"Kelsie, she can't get hurt again. We can't let her."

"Daddy's been gone for a few years now, Jamie. I guess Mama wants someone to talk to and be around."

"Who is he, Kelsie? What does he look like? I can't believe this."

"Jamie, don't say a word to her. Mama will talk about it when she's ready."

"I'm tired of secrets. Who are we really? Everything I thought I knew about us is wrong. Why are things like this? Please, tell me the truth, is there anything else I don't know?"

"Kelsie, was I adopted?"

"No, no, Jamie, stop it! You were not adopted. You look so much like Daddy, how could you think that? I've got to go meet someone, but I'll be back."

"Who are you meeting? Is it another guy, Kelsie?" She stands there, refusing to answer. "Well, be careful! What should I tell Mama if she asks?"

"Tell her I had to meet up with someone from work to talk about switching schedules."

"No, Kelsie, I'm not lying for you."

"It's not a lie unless you told her I was meeting up with someone other than a coworker. The less you know the better. Now, I have to go. And you, Jamie Annette Moore, do not open your mouth about what we talked about."

"I won't. You know I won't." I sigh heavily as I leave her room and shut the door behind me.

∞∞∞

June 1989

I've been watching Mama for a while now, trying to see if something's changed with her. I wonder what sort of man she's seeing. I ask her if she's okay and she says she's great. She even said she was going to lunch with Ms. Mae from work on Saturday. The other night when she left, going God knows where, she pulled out her old perfume she'd packed away after Daddy died. I knew then she was going to see him and that it was more serious than I thought.

I finally got up the courage to talk to Mama and she admitted to dating the man she introduced me to at the store, Steve. She likes him. He just lost his house and has been down on his luck after losing his manufacturing job when the plant closed. He just started at a new company, but he'd already fallen so far behind on his house payments and had to sell it rather than lose it all together. He wants to get an apartment of his own, but he'd rather help her some and save up a little more so he can move into a nicer place close by. She offered him a place here for a few months. When she told me that, I felt like time froze. Some man I've only seen twice is coming to live with us. Sure, we need help, but not that kind of help. Mama told me to calm down after the look of shock came over my face. She asked me to try to understand. With Kelsie leaving, we'll need the extra money for graduation, college, and other things as they come up. She assured me he'd only be here for a couple of months, and no more than three. The thought of a strange man living with us terrifies me. I don't know him. Beyond that, this is my daddy's house! It seems so wrong that he'll be sleeping under my Daddy's roof. Where will Mr. Steve sleep—with her? The thought disgusts me.

Kelsie and I were talking this morning. She's as angry as I am, but she told Mama outright what she felt, and now she can't wait to leave. She's upset that I'll be here, though, and said she would take me with her if she could. Mama's very upset with Kelsie, but somewhere deep inside she knows what Kelsie was saying is true.

∞∞∞

September 1989

Mr. Steve arrived with three bags, an old suitcase, and one rundown pillow that should be in the trash. He spent the first few weeks sleeping on the couch, but last night Mama told him to get into bed with her. I wish she hadn't said it where I could hear. It's repulsive to think of him in my daddy's bed. I don't know what she sees in him. He isn't the nicest looking man. His hair looks like he's stuck in the 70s, his face is sunburnt red, and he has the driest curl I'd ever seen.

I haven't been sleeping well. I feel too uneasy sleeping while he's here. How can I trust a man I don't know? What if he kills us in our sleep? I've been spending the night in Kelsie's room—her bed is big enough to share. She hates it, but she understands why I'm doing it. How could Mama do this to us? After school tomorrow, I'm going to tell Mama that I'm finding a job. If he's staying here because of money, then I'll work and go to school if I have to. Maybe if she sees me being more responsible and helping out she'll get him out of here.

I don't know my mother anymore. She acts as if nothing's wrong. She's been okay though since he's been here. She's alive, but not like I remember her being with Daddy. She's a new person, a stranger. The betrayal beneath my skin itches. I love my mama, but I don't know if she can make good choices anymore. I have to focus on graduation and I have to deal with all of this. Kelsie's upset all the time and more determined to leave no matter what; she's saving every penny she can and working longer hours too.

I pray my Daddy's listening. Maybe he can help us somehow.

Mr. Steve is disturbing. I'll never feel good about having him in our home. Sometimes, he goes days without speaking to Kelsie or me—he just ignores us whenever Mama isn't around. He stares sometimes too, making us uncomfortable. Kelsie and I get a lock for my door so I can sleep at night. I keep a kitchen knife under my pillow too, just in case.

I've tried to talk to Mama, but we haven't had a real conversation since he moved in. I don't think God is happy with us. Mama never goes to church anymore and Kelsie works on Sundays, so I've been going alone. Every Sunday, I walk to church alone along the same path we used to take as a family. I know each house on the block by memory. I think about the families who no longer live here and the unfamiliar families who've moved in recently. I feel safer outside in the neighborhood than I do in my own house no matter how foggy the air or dark the night. Even when the fog's so thick and gray that I can't see my own feet, I still feel safer outside.

On the way to church, I passed by Ms. Marie's house and saw her gardeners tending to the yard. She was out there with her rose bushes, which are looking pretty as ever. That lady has folks cutting her yard professionally, but she takes care of those flowers like they're her babies. They're always so nice to see. Even though I'd rather we went to church as a family, I like walking alone and having some time to think things through. I'm looking forward to college; it'll be so different. I can't let myself get too wrapped up in the past.

Church usually doesn't make me cry, but it did today. After the service, I went to the front of the church for prayer. I wanted Pastor Andrews to pray for my family, especially Mama. The folks at church know Mama's got a new man living in our house. I'm so embarrassed; it feels like the whole entire world knows. I didn't expect their looks of pity, and feeling like the whole church had their eyes on me. Church has always been a safe place for me; I never felt judged like that before. Pastor Andrews caught me before I left.

He looked me in the eyes and whispered, "God never leaves or forsakes us. Your mama will be okay. She's a strong woman who's just trying to find her way."

I thanked him and immediately walked out. I couldn't look back. It'll be a long time before I go back there again. I can't bare the embarrassment of my mother's choices.

Chapter Five

Summer 1990

I finally got through high school. It's been hard for me, having to be a student and an adult at once. I can't say I had an easy senior year. Most of my classmates worried about what they were wearing to prom, while I was concerned about sleeping peacefully at night. I enjoy spending time with Kelsie before she leaves in a few weeks, but I'm busy getting ready for school. I wish I could afford to live on campus, but I wouldn't leave Mama right now even if I could.

Today, I enrolled in my classes and took the freshman tour of the campus at Rice University. Mama agreed to sign the waiver allowing me to live at home. Otherwise, I couldn't afford the campus living expenses. This is hard when you are figuring things out for yourself. People were everywhere and the other students were walking around, looking as lost as I was. But the difference was they were all with their parents. Even though I know Daddy's spirit is with me, I'm here alone. Mama had to work and Kelsie's getting ready to leave for California. It's normal for me, though. I'm not a bit bothered by it. I have to handle my business and ask as many questions as possible. The campus is so beautiful. I needed a change and I got it. I wanted to get as far away from my house as I could without leaving the city completely. Coming out here a few days a week will be worth it. I don't have to be at home all the time, which is good. I'd rather not be around that man as often as I can.

∞∞∞

Autumn 1990

Everyone I've seen seems so refined and proper; I feel so awkward. But I'm here because the college approved my application. That means I belong here, just like everyone else. I have a lot to do to be prepared for this part of my life.

Between school and helping Mama out at the store, I'm so tired. College is going to take some getting use to. I'm worried about keeping my grades up and staying focused, but as time goes on, I can't help but want more fun in my life. I've been hearing so much about clubs and extracurricular activities around school—I feel like I've missed so much. I guess having little exposure to that stuff keeps me out of trouble. Just the other day, one of my study partners asked me to go with her to a party her friend was hosting. I said no for many reasons, but mostly because I knew what kind of party it was. I told her mixing alcohol and coeds just screams disaster.

She gave me this unforgettable look, rolled her eyes, and said, "Jamie, I will never ask you out to a party again."

I apologized and said, "Sarah, I'm just not interested in that kind of thing."

She said, "Girl, you're too old-fashioned for your own good. Live a little."

Mama is doing well and Steve is just Steve. He has been working late, so I try to be in my room with the door closed before he gets in. If there is anything I need to say to Mama, I say it while he's out of the house. That's the system I created to avoid him. I think I'm thirsting for my own life.

Chapter Six

Autumn 1991

Time is flying by Kelsie's been in California for over a year now. We talk some, but mostly write back and forth. I miss her more than I ever thought I could. Steve still lives with us, no surprise there. A few weeks turned into a few months, now it's been almost two years. It still bothers me—he's rude and hateful as ever, but like always only shows his true colors when Mama isn't around.

Kelsie and Steve were like oil and water when she was here. They got into screaming arguments all the time. I tried to stay out of it, but I knew she was leaving and I would have to deal with him after she was gone. He thought she was too disrespectful, and should have moved out of the house a long time ago. He would say the meanest things to her.

I remember one night when he started in on her after she'd come home late. He said she was sleeping with every guy who would take her out and she was getting all used up. Kelsie got right in his face and said he was only living in our house because our mama felt sorry for his pathetic self. He balled up his fist like he was going to hit her. I remember seeing it shaking at his side. Steve called her a dreamer and said she might have thought she was all that, but she was really less than nothing.

Before she slammed her bedroom door, he said coldly, "Don't be surprised if you go all the way to California and your nice, important Daddy ships your half-baked butt back to Texas." What kind of person would say something like that? Steve is as horrible as they come. I wish I could tell Mama the things he says. Better yet, I wish she'd believe me.

Once Kelsie left, he started in on me. He said we were disappointments and that Mama is too good of a person to tell us the truth. He keeps telling her we don't treat her right—that we don't give her enough respect. Then he turns to me and says I should be ashamed of myself for my behavior. What behavior? Taking care of her? I get so angry sometimes when I think about how Kelsie was able to get away from here; I wish I could leave too but the semester only started last month and I need to focus on school. College is wonderful, but it's not enough to make me happy. I wish Mama were strong enough to see Steve for who he really is. His attitude is unbearable at times and I just can't take much more of it.

Loneliness Within

September 21, 1991

Hey Kels,

How are you? How's school at USC? I'm sure everything is great on your end. School's an escape for me. I'm looking forward to getting out of here for good one day. Mama's doing great, and you-know-who is the same. He refuses to even look at me. I'll talk to him and he just nods his head if he does anything at all. What the heck is wrong with him, Kels? He asks me why I don't move closer to school. What kind of question is that? He knows we can't afford a dorm or apartment, but he still wants me to move out. Sometimes he just says, "Jamie, get the hell out! It's time for you to go!" I hate him. I know Daddy would say not to feel that way about anyone, but I do. I so badly want to tell Mama who he really is, but he has her fooled completely. She's happy, I guess, and I don't want to ruin that for her.

There is so much I want to say, but you have your life. Be happy, Kelsie. I love you so much. I hope we can visit you next year.

Over and out!

I'm enjoying my classes. It takes me away from this house mentally. I stay busy to keep the peace. After speaking long distance over the phone with Kelsie last week and writing her yesterday, I feel a little better. It's so funny that she's into medical administration. I've never

44

known her to be interested in science or heath care. But since she wants to work with her dad in his clinic, it makes sense to get a degree in that field. I still can't believe her dad has his own clinic. I bet I could ask him a lot of questions that would help me get through my Biology tests. She's so lucky to have someone she can call 'dad.' I miss Daddy every day.

She's dating someone new. She wants Mama and me to come visit over the summer. She even said she'll pay for it. She sends Mama money every month and paid for most of my books this semester. The clothes she sends me are amazing too; they look like they are straight off the racks of the finest boutiques in Beverly Hills. She said folks are fabulous there, very free spirited and carefree. But, Mama and I were watching the news the other night and there's been a lot of racial tension in California. Kelsie doesn't seem the least bit bothered by it, though. I guess she isn't forced to face those issues where she lives, but the black community in and around Los Angeles is outraged.

I'm glad she's doing so well. It's good to know I can count on my sister to help me even when she's across the country. She always knows what I need and what I'll look good in—and I must look good because people compliment me all the time. The last package she sent had a lot of vibrant colors. Its fall and the bright reds are banging. I'm focused and prepared. I've been trying to take care of my appearance more; I think I did my hair some justice today. It's easier to manage when I can straighten it. I appreciate everything she's doing for us, but I still wish Kelsie was here.

Loneliness Within

Today, on the bus ride home, I noticed a sign on the side of the road that said, "Church on the Hill needs volunteers! You're invited to rejoice with us! Let's win back our kids!" I've been thinking about it since then and I can't help but wonder what it's about. I haven't been to church since the time I was so embarrassed. Church people can be cruel and intimidating, but they never see themselves that way.

Maybe if I find another church, Mama would go with me. I've been thinking she might be too embarrassed or too ashamed to go back to the church we went to for so long, especially now that she has a live-in situation. I know our church would eat her alive. Steve isn't the church-going type. When I first brought it up, you would have thought he was allergic to wood pews by his reaction. I think I'll take a look at that church next time I'm on the bus and if it feels right, I'll sign up to volunteer. It'll help me occupy some of my free time. Lord knows I have enough spare time. I don't want to be at home.

∞∞∞

Last night, I couldn't stop thinking about visiting the church I saw on the street sign. I decided to head there this morning. Maybe I'll meet some people, even make some friends. The sign said they needed volunteers for the youth outreach program, which sounds like something I could do. I finally made it to the church. It's a lot busier than I thought it would be, and I'm glad the bus ride isn't

46

very long—and there's a stop just a block away. Everyone is rushing around doing this and that. A feeling came over me when I walked in door; it kind of reminds me of Daddy. This just feels right. I know he'd want me to do this. I'm going to give it a chance. I'm not sure where the offices are, so I stop and ask one of the little kids running around, playing in the halls, where I might find the adults. She points me down a narrow hallway.

There's an open door and I can hear a man talking on the phone. I softly knock on the door before poking my head in. The office is comfortable and clean, though his desk is an organized mess. As the man piles donations into a box, he waves me in and quickly wraps up his phone call.

"Come in. Sorry about that. Oh, before I forget, let me put this box away and I'll be right with you."

"Okay, that's fine," I say, taking a look around the small office.

"All right, I'm all done you are Ms.—?"

"Jamie Moore." I stick out my hand and he shakes it. His hands are nice and warm, handshake firm.

"Ms. Moore, I'm sorry to keep you waiting. I'm Minister Jace Lawrence. How can I help you?"

"Nice to meet you, Minster Lawrence."

"Please call me Jace," he says, smiling.

"Okay, Jace, I wanted to know more about volunteering with the church. I go to school on the bus route and saw your sign. I thought I'd like to get involved."

"Oh, that's wonderful. In what capacity?"

"I'm not sure. I think I saw something about your youth outreach. That sounds interesting."

"Oh, that's great! Then I'm just the right person to talk to. I lead the youth ministry here. We need all the help we can get. Let me take down your information and I'll call you. I also coordinate the program. It shouldn't be more than a few days." He paused and smiled genuinely. "We have so much need, Ms. Moore. Let me show you around the church."

"I would love that."

He is nice and passionate about what he's doing. He had me fill out a form. He never stopped talking about how wonderful the people are at the church and how he is so blessed to doing something he loves every day. This is a very nice church and they take very good care of it.

"Well, this hall leads back to my office where we started. Thank you for agreeing to volunteer; I will have your volunteer form processed, it's been a pleasure meeting you."

"It's nice meeting you as well, Jace. I'll wait to hear from you."

"May God be with you." I smile and close the office door behind me as I leave.

It was easier than I thought it would be. I need to remember to tell Mama to let me know when the church calls. I walk out of the church and head back to the bus stop, thinking all the while about how well put together Jace was. He's as tall as daddy was—around 5'11 or so with the curliest waves I've ever seen on a man. He had gorgeous chestnut brown eyes that matched his skin tone. But, thinking about attractive men isn't why I went there. I guess I wasn't expecting to meet someone so close in age who looks so nice. It's getting late, but I know it was worth it. I think I can still catch a bus back home, even though I hate to return to my lonely existence. People look at me in class and around school as if I have everything put together. If they only knew how scared and lonely I am inside, they might think differently.

As I walk up to the stop, I notice a woman sleeping on the ground in a shadowed doorway. I think of my father and dig a couple of dollars out of my wallet, making sure I still have enough for bus fare. I can spare a little. I don't know her story, but everyone has one. I hope she's okay and finds a way to get up from here one day.

I can't wait to start volunteering. Jace was kind. He didn't seem much older than me, but he's running the outreach for his church. Look at me trying to find my way in this world and there he is, already knowing what he wants and doing it. He sure was nice looking though, but that's not what I should be thinking about. He's a man of God.

∞∞∞

I'm trying not to let the things Steve says bother me. The other day he said, "You sure are getting old to not have ever had a man. What's wrong with you? Aren't you tired of being the only one alone?" I ignored him and pretended I was watching TV. But, I've let it fester deep inside my thoughts. He's right; I am alone. I do need someone to talk to, someone who will take me on dates or just get me out of this house occasionally.

The guys at school are so simple minded. They only want to party and date every girl they see. You can't take them seriously. Their conversation consists of what parties they're going to, which women they've been with, and how drunk they can get on the weekend. I need a guy to take me places I haven't been before. I want someone who will dazzle me with his maturity and knowledge. Some of the young women in my classes invite me to hang out, but I feel like an outsider. I'd like to live on campus, so I could feel like I'm a part of the community, but I'm too poor. I just can't afford to hang out like they do and spend money frivolously. Besides, I take the bus, which limits when and where I can go. I wouldn't dare ask them to take me all the way home. I've realized just how lonely I am. I've never been very good with people, especially compared to Kelsie. It didn't take her any time at all to find someone in California. I used to fill a lot of my free time hanging with her, but now I only have myself.

It's been three days since I went to the church and Mama says no one has called for me. I hope they call soon. This morning the bus is packed with people heading out to start their day. I look and feel beautiful because I've been fixing my hair just the way Kelsie said I should. It's been windy out and the hairstyle looks good even after I stood out in the wind. I'm a woman and I need to look like one. No man will take me seriously if I look like a plain Jane school girl with a ponytail, dressed like a kid. I'm sticking with this new look. Maybe someone worth something will notice me. Kelsie always refused to leave the house looking any kind of way because she said she could meet her prince charming at any moment. I get it now. After all these years of her telling me, I finally understand how important appearance is. It's worked for her and it can for me.

The woman next to me jostles my bag as I try to get out the bus door at my stop. I step out of the bus and onto the sidewalk, already digging into my bag for my compact as I head to class. Kelsie said I should always check to make sure my gloss is still on my lips before going anywhere, whether it's class or out to dinner. I keep walking as I struggle to find the little mirror in the depths of my school bag. I turn the corner and bump square into a man walking down the street, spilling his papers and coffee all over the ground.

"I'm so sorry, sir! Here, let me help," I crouch down and start picking up any dry papers I can as he picks up what's left of his coffee. "I can't believe I knocked all your things down; I wasn't looking where I was going."

"No, I'm sorry for not paying attention to such a beautiful lady such as yourself. What's your name, miss...?"

"Me?" I ask, smiling as a blush creeps over my cheeks. "I was just looking for something in my bag, please forgive me."

"No, it's okay it's partly my fault too. So, what's your name?"

"I'm Jamie."

"You from around here?"

"Not really, I'm a student here—" The campus clock chimes noon and I momentarily panic. I've only got fifteen minutes to get all the way across campus and prep for a quiz. "I'm sorry again, but I'm late meeting my classmates to study. I've gotta go." I stand up, adjusting my bag, and heading off toward my class.

He calls out, "Before you leave and I lose you forever, could I talk you to again?"

I turn, blink rapidly, deeply surprised, and smile. "Sure, that would be nice. I'll be out of class in two hours. We could meet here?"

"That sounds lovely," he says grinning and giving me a subtle once-over.

Loneliness Within

I stumble slightly over my own feet in my haste to turn and get to class. "Sorry again about what happened. Bye!" I whisper over my shoulder.

Class goes by in a blur and I can't remember anything my professor said. The test? Well, let's just say I'll be lucky to receive a passing grade. I've been thinking about *him*. He was so nice and well dressed and oh my, did he smell like a million dollars. I can't help but wonder if he's going to be out there, waiting for me. I'm so nervous. As I approach the corner by the bookstore and bus stop where I ran into him, I don't see him anywhere. I don't know why I expected him to wait for me for more than two hours. That was silly of me. I guess I might see him again, but chances are I won't. All this lip-gloss and excitement is just a waste of time. I sigh and turn the corner, heading back down the block to catch the bus home.

A hand clasps my elbow gently and I quickly turn around, startled. "Hey, pretty lady, did you think I'd pass on the chance to talk to you again?"

I can feel a grin spreading across my face and I can't stop it. "Hi, I didn't see you, so I figured you got caught up in something and couldn't make it."

"I did have some business in the area, but I said to myself 'Daniel, you need to go back to see her again—she's one of a kind.'"

"Really? Just like that, huh?" *Daniel*, I like his name. It's solid and sweet.

"Yes, just like that. Can I take you where you're going?"

"Oh no, I'm sorry—you're very nice and all, but I don't know you well enough for that."

"Okay, would you just give me a moment to lock up my car and put some money in the meter? Then I can at least walk with you."

"Sure, but I'm only walking down to the bus stop."

"That's fine. It would be my pleasure to accompany you. We can chat while we wait." He jogs lightly over to his new black Cadillac, locks it, and drops two quarters into the meter, buying him about 30 minutes. He quickly returns to my side and we walk slowly down the block.

"I don't normally do things like this, but somethings telling me you're really special, Jamie."

"You remember my name?"

"Of course, I couldn't forget it, and may I say to you have an untouched innocence about you. It's breathtaking." I must look surprised or slightly put off because he immediately continues. "I must apologize for my candid honesty. I don't mean to make you uncomfortable. Please, let me start over—how long have you been in school here?"

"I'm in my second year."

"Oh, nice. Sophomore year is good—still fresh enough to be interested in what you're doing without all the discomfort of learning the campus and how things work. What are you studying?"

"I'm a biology major."

"That's different, definitely not something I hear every day. You must be extremely smart." The bus stop has just has a few people waiting. I sit down on the bench, careful not to snag my clothing on its rough wood surface. He sits close to me, but not uncomfortably so.

"No, not really, or, well, I don't think so. I do well in my classes and I like taking care of people. I want to learn how to fix them."

"You want to be a doctor? That's impressive." I see my bus cresting the slight hill and stand up, moving closer to the street.

"It's been nice talking to you, but that's my bus coming."

"Can I please call you?" he asks.

"Sure, I'd like that." I drag a scrap piece of paper out of my bag and scribble the home phone onto it. "Here, if no one answers just leave a message. It was nice meeting you, Daniel." I say as I climb onto the bus.

"Bye Jamie, I'll be calling you soon!"

I settle into one of the coveted single seats toward the middle of the bus and try to calm the butterflies in my stomach. What just happened? Not only did he come back, but he was driving a new shiny Cadillac. I can't believe he waited with me at a bus stop just to chat. He didn't have to do that. Okay, I don't want to mess this up, but I also shouldn't put too much into it. I need to be mature. I am shaking with excitement. The butterflies won't go away. Is this what love at first sight feels like? I close my eyes and take a deep breath. He probably thinks I'm too young, too inexperienced. He's way too much for me anyway, but I can't stop thinking about him.

∞∞∞

Turning off the shower, I hear my mama holler for me from just outside the bathroom door, telling me to come see her as soon as I'm done. I grab a towel, quickly dry off, and put on my clothes. I head into the kitchen where she's doing the dishes. She looks up and gestures toward the phone.

"Jamie, a guy called for you when you were in the shower."

My breath catches in my chest. "Did he leave a name?" I ask excitedly.

"I don't remember, but he left his number. It's over there on the counter." I dash across the room, grab the little piece of paper, and tuck it into my pocket.

"Steve and I are leaving for a few hours; I think we're going out for dinner."

"Okay, sounds good," I say distractedly. The butterflies have returned. I'm so nervous and excited. I can't believe he called so soon—we only met this afternoon. I thought I'd be waiting a couple of days before I'd hear from him. But he seemed so interested in me. I pace back and forth in my room before picking up the phone and dialing the number he left.

"Hello?" A deep, smooth voice answers.

"Hi, this is Jamie. I'm returning your call."

"Yes, of course. Hello, Ms. Jamie. This is Jace Lawrence from the Church on the Hill."

"Oh, yes, hello." I couldn't keep the disappointment out of my voice.

"I'm sorry, you sound disappointed—am I calling at a bad time?"

"No, Reverend Lawrence, not at all. I apologize, I simply thought this was about something else."

"I understand, and please call me Jace."

"Okay, Jace it is."

"I apologize for taking so long to get back with you, but I'm currently the only one running the youth

57

outreach program and it can be a bit overwhelming at times."

"Don't worry about it, Jace."

"Ms. Jamie, I called because we could really use your help this Saturday. I know it's a bit last minute, but we need volunteers—several people had to back out just yesterday evening due to personal issues. Anyway, we're going door-to-door on Saturday asking young people to come out to our annual upcoming Thanksgiving food drive. Would you like to join us?"

"Absolutely, I'd love to help out."

"Great! That's wonderful. I'll see you then. We will meet at the church at 4 p.m. and it shouldn't take more than a few hours of your evening. Is that okay?"

"Yes, that sounds perfect. I'll see you then."

"Thank you so much, Ms. Jamie. It was great speaking with you." I say goodbye and have to resist slamming the phone into its cradle. I can't believe I thought Daniel was calling so soon. Well, at least I'm not going to sit here all weekend waiting on Daniel's call and feeling sick while I'm stuck watching Steve and Mama cuddling. I have actual plans—something more than just schoolwork and watching old reruns on TV.

∞∞∞

Loneliness Within

The bus this morning is unusually quiet for a Friday. The sun is waiting to blaze the morning breeze away. As I get off the bus, I start walking toward my classes when I spot Daniel's car parked near where we ran into each other on Monday. Excitement and nerves rush through me, but I keep my chin high and refuse to look his direction. But, I can't help but to notice out of the corner of my eye that he's inside the car with the windows up and the engine running. I want to pretend I don't see him. I'm not going to be one of those offended people who can't accept it when someone isn't interested in them. I don't want him to have to make up a reason why he never called. I'll just ignore him. I'm not far from his car when he climbs out, all smiles and expensive cologne radiating from his pores.

"Hello, pretty lady." I momentarily panic, *Is he talking to me?* I can't help but make eye contact. I stop walking and turn to him, searching his eyes for an answer.

"Hi Daniel, how are you?"

"Good," he reaches into his car through the open passenger side window and removes a small, but lovely bouquet. "These are for you."

"Roses? You got me roses? They're beautiful. You didn't have to do this."

"I did. I lost your number that night. Since you were here Monday, I thought I might be able to catch you today since it's the end of the week. Most classes are Monday, Wednesday, and Friday. I just got back in town and my luck was right—here you are."

59

"Were you waiting here long?"

"No, not really, but I was really hoping to see you."

"Not that I'm not flattered, but why?"

"Can I be honest?" I nod. "I believe you were meant for me."

I'm slightly taken back by his confidence. "You don't know me."

"I know enough to know you're one of a kind. I'm a very determined man, pretty lady."

I look at the roses and then back up at him. "Yes, I can see that."

"I hope it doesn't bother you. I know I'm coming on strong, but I've never met someone who instantly caught my attention like you have."

"No, it's just that…I don't know what to say," I smile up at him.

"No, be honest. Tell me what you're thinking." I hesitate and then gesture to his suit and fancy car.

"You seem like a very busy man, but you took the time to wait for me and give me roses to apologize for not calling me. That's…" I laugh quietly. "That's something out of a romance novel." He smirks slightly and shifts his weight, somehow making every movement charming.

"This isn't a book. It's really happening."

I hike my bag further onto my shoulder as it slips slightly. He watches my every motion. "Never mind that. I would like to take you to a late lunch after your classes."

I don't think I have anything after class, but something makes me cautious. "I don't know I'm just very…"

"Okay, tell you what, why don't we just go to the sandwich cafe on the corner. It's on campus; so we can walk and I'll buy you lunch. How does that sound?"

I breathe a sigh of relief. I really didn't want to have to turn down a date because I wasn't comfortable going somewhere alone with him yet. "That sounds great."

"Then we have a date."

"My class runs until 2 p.m."

"I'll meet you back here in three hours."

∞∞∞∞

Daniel is the most confident, good-looking man I've ever laid eyes on.

"How long is your bus ride?" he asks, sitting across from me in the booth.

I see this cafe when I get off the bus all the time, but never paid any attention to it until today. The waitress is kind. She told us they're famous for their bagels and famous brewed coffee. The place was packed and after tasting my sandwhich, I can see why.

"I ride from the southern side of Houston."

"You sure are a long ways from home, but you're determined. You must be to come all the way out here on the city bus."

"It's so different out here. I like that it takes me away from my normal life. The ride and the change of pace is a blessing to me."

I quickly lost track of time and we talked for hours. Going to class with roses was a little embarrassing, but I still can't get over that he waited for me and said he believed we were meant to be.

"I hope you don't mind." He takes my hand from the table and pulls it to him, wrapping his warm palm against mine. His nails are well-kept, maybe even manicured. He's definitely not a man who works with his hands.

"No, I don't mind," I say, blushing with inexperience. His eyes peer through me, directly into my mind, as if he was searching for hidden secrets. It's a bit intimidating, but he's very affectionate. He grabbed my hands several more times and I let him.

Money isn't a problem for him. He has own business he retired from the military a couple of years ago. His mother and father have both passed; they died while he was overseas. Their deaths deeply troubled him; emptiness fell over his eyes when he spoke of them.

"Everyone handles things on their own time. I can tell you were very close to them."

He clears his throat. "That's a subject I stay away from normally. I was always told to keep conversations general and refrain from too much personal business. It could come back to haunt you later."

He says he found it difficult to connect with people outside of a few very committed friends he calls his family since then. I completely understand what he means. I tell him about Daddy and we instantly bond.

"What about when you're out on date?" I ask.

"Like now? I've been talking about me too long and that takes away from me noticing how beautiful you are at this moment." He swiftly and firmly controls the conversation from that moment on. I don't mind. I'm comforted by all of his attention.

Later, he invites me to a movie and dinner Saturday. I say I can, but I need to call Jace and let him know something came up. I feel so bad, but I'd much rather be with Daniel than knocking on doors. I need to talk to Kelsie; I only have until Saturday to find something to wear. I've also gotta get my homework done so I won't have any distractions or worries during the date. Oh, wow, I'm so happy. My very first date with a man! I hope I don't ruin it.

When I tell Mama I'm going on a date with the most amazing man named Daniel, we're in the kitchen.

She says, "Jamie, you've never been on a date with a man before. I want you to make sure you know the man before you fall for him, honey."

I say, "I know him well enough for now, Mama. He's good and he knows what he wants and is very mature."

"How old is he? Is he married—has he ever been? Does he have children?" I shuffle my feet and tell her I didn't know any of those questions. "I told you before, everybody ain't good that looks good." I know what she's thinking, but I explain that it's just a date—I'm not marrying him. We're just getting to know each other.

"I see the truth in those eyes of yours, Jamie. I know you're taking a liking to him much too fast. I can see it."

"Mama, please don't act this way. Just be happy for me. I'm happy."

"Yeah and I'm just trying to make sure you stay that way."

I wish I knew why she was being like this. I thought she'd be happy for me. I'm finally embracing being a woman and doing adult things. I leave the kitchen because I don't want to be disrespectful. Tonight, I'm going to sleep happy and there's nothing anyone can do about it.

∞∞∞

Saturday is finally here. I drag myself out of bed, fully intending on having a nice, slow day until I need to get ready for my date with Daniel, until I glance at my calendar. Today's date is circled and I've written *Food Drive Outreach*. I forgot to call Jace. I promised him I'd help out this afternoon. I can go and be back in time to get dressed for that fine man who's taking me out tonight. I'll ask Mama to drive me to church. I know how she hates to drive, but Jace will have to bring me home early. I can't chance not being ready and dressed when Daniel gets here. Oh, time is not on my side today. I said I'd volunteer, so here's my chance.

I arrive later than I would have liked, but there are still a lot of people around and it was still going strong. I work for a few hours before I apologized to Jace and ask if he wouldn't mind taking me home a little early. There's still so much work to do, but I'm so focused on my date and I've already done a lot, so I'm definitely not leaving them in a jam if I head out a bit early. Jace agrees to take me home, which means I don't have to waste time with the bus. He has a nice, modest car and keeps it very clean.

"Thank you so much, sir. I'm sorry I couldn't stay longer and help more, but I have plans and I just can't be late." He pulls out of the parking lot and onto the road, heading in the direction of my house.

"It's just Jace and it isn't a problem. You don't have to be so formal with me. I was just glad to see you come out and help, so thank you for that."

"Oh, no, thank you for the opportunity, and the ride home. I know folks are going to be wondering where you went."

"No, I told the brother from the adult ministry where I was going. I said I'd be back soon. Why don't you tell me a bit about yourself, Ms. Jamie?" He quickly glanced at me and smiled.

"Well, I'm a sophomore in college at Rice University. I have a sister who lives in California. I live with my mother and her boyfriend. My father, who was an amazing man, died several years ago. It hasn't been the same without him."

"Oh, I'm sorry to hear that," he says with genuine concern. It's so rare to hear a person talk that way. It's refreshing.

"It's okay. Every day is a little easier to bear, but a big part of me will never really be over it. Anyway, I was raised in church, but stopped going as much when my mother stopped too after my dad's death. But I believe in God and I love him. It's how my father raised us. I think finding this church is a good thing for me. I want to make my father proud."

Jace is silent for a bit, just listening to me until we pull into my driveway.

"Well, I hope you make it to where you're going on time. If it's okay, Ms. Jamie, I'd like to call you sometime."

"I should have plenty of time since you could drive me and I didn't have to take the bus. And, yes, feel free to call anytime. Thank you again for bringing me home."

"You're welcome." I gather up my purse and climb out of the car, but before I can shut the door, he speaks again.

"Oh, Ms. Jamie, after Thanksgiving we'll be starting our Christmas outreach. I'd love for you to help, if you're able. A group of us go out for a couple of days and walk the neighborhood inviting young people to the Christmas service and putting up fliers advertising it."

"Sure, I would love to help. Just call me and remind me, okay?" He nods.

"Until next time, Ms. Jamie."

Jace pulls away after I unlock the door and get inside. He's such a kind soul, but I can't get Daniel out of my mind. Some part of me thinks Jace might be a better fit for me. I think Daddy would have liked someone like him more, but I just don't think of him that way. He doesn't give me butterflies in my stomach like just thinking about Daniel does. Maybe Mama's right, though? I should ask more questions about Daniel's personal life, but it just seems so soon. We've only gone for lunch. He wasn't wearing a ring, so that's good, I guess. I'll find out the rest later, hopefully soon.

I'm so thankful Mama and Steve aren't around when Daniel picks me up today. I don't want to turn Daniel off with Steve's hovering and Mama's skepticism and thousand questions about his intentions. We went to the movies and then had dinner at a wonderful barbecue place across town. It was a fancy place—candles on the tables, low lighting, even a live band. I felt a little under dressed, but Daniel told me not to worry about it. We had such a nice evening. We didn't talk much. Daniel seemed hypnotized by the band. He wanted to dance, but I didn't feel comfortable drawing attention to myself when I wasn't dressed right. He gently grabbed my hand under the table and said we're definitely dancing next time we had dinner there. Before we left, we went to the back. He knows the owner, I guess. They all greeted him with a smile. Everyone knew him by name. He seems to be very popular from what I can see. He knew people at the cafe, at the restaurant, and even at the movie theater. I love walking into a room with him; he draws everyone's attention without doing a thing, especially from women. They all look at him, but he pays them no attention. I can't believe that out of everyone, he wants to be with me. Who is this man?

Chapter Seven

Winter 1992

The past few months have been a whirlwind. Daniel's been so good to me. He showers me with gifts and always wants me around him. I see him at least a few times a week. He said I'm like a feeling of security he hasn't felt in years. The other night we went out late to a dinner party. He said the men there were either current or future business partners. We met in a really nice hotel suite. I can't believe people live like that, where money is no object. I'm not sure who these people were, but they seemed rich and important to me. I followed his lead and stayed quiet most of the time. I noticed the other ladies and how they worked the room, but I smiled nodded a little and stayed by Daniel's side.

On the way home, he said he wants to take care of me. God knows I need someone to do that. He's always busy though, even when we're together. Every time we go out, he's constantly receiving pages and calls; he's got so much going on. I've never seen anyone so busy. I try not to let it bother me, and he definitely doesn't make me feel like I'm being ignored. I just want to try to fit in, like I belong with him and his friends, even though I know deep down I don't. I've never been around people like this before, inside of fancy hotel suites. I'm a poor young woman in college living with my mother trying to find my way in life. He keeps telling me not to worry about anything—that he'll take care of all my needs.

On the way home after our date just late last night, he said he was going out of town for a few weeks and that when he came back he wants to take me somewhere really special for a night on the town. I hope I can find something that looks good enough to wear for him. I'll ask Mama if I could help out at the store a little more for some extra money so I can buy myself a new dress. He's a well-dressed man and I want to have something fancy enough to impress him. Oh, who am I fooling? I can't afford expensive clothes.

∞∞∞∞

I've been helping out at the church here and there with Jace. He's become a good friend. We have a lot in common. He is close to his mother and father. He was raised in church and his brother, who he's close to, lives out of town like Kelsie. We're both the youngest in our family. Jace gets me. He knows and understands my relationship with my mom better than anyone. But, I stood him up yesterday. I must admit I like volunteering with him, but I've been so tired from spending time with Daniel and trying to keep up with school, I just didn't have the energy to help out this week. The worst part was that I completely forgot to call him to apologize for backing out. I hope they had enough people volunteering so I wasn't missed. I really enjoy working with everyone; I feel just awful.

∞∞∞∞

I was able to save up and buy the dress I wanted for tonight. I spent every dime I made at the store for the last two weeks on it along with a purse and earrings. I'm so excited for our night out. I hear Daniel's car pulling into our driveway as I give myself one last look in the mirror. I look amazing. Daniel promised something special, so I took extra care tonight. It took me two hours to straighten my hair so it shines and blows in the wind just like the first day we met. I'm so happy to see him after he's been gone for the past few weeks. Mama's finally going to meet him tonight.

I can hear him knocking on the door. I need to act like I'm not ready, though Lord knows I've been ready since this afternoon. *Okay, Jamie, get it together—breathe.* I walk out the back room to try to make an entrance.

"Mama," I say as I slowly walk in, showing off my new dress, "I see you've met Daniel. Daniel, this beautiful woman is my sweet mother, Mrs. Diana Moore."

"Yes, she was just telling me that you're her special baby—a different kind of young woman than most, very honest and caring. I told her I couldn't agree more."

"Mama," I say admonishingly, embarrassed by her praise, "Thank you." I step all the way back and stand next to Daniel, who stops me at arm's length and looks me over respectfully.

"Jamie, wow, you look as beautiful as ever—just amazing. I have something special for you in the car."

"Well, aren't you full of surprises."

"I try to be," he says sliding a hand to my lower back. "It was nice meeting you, Mrs. Moore."

"I'll see you later, Mama," I pull her close for a quick hug and whisper in her ear, "Wish me luck." She gives me a small, polite smile and closes the door behind us. We approach his car and Daniel grabs a box out of the trunk.

"This is for you," he says as he hands it to me.

"This is a big box what is it?" I ask as I open it up. "Oh! This is a beautiful red dress!" I pull it out of a large white box with a lovely bow before holding it up against me. "It's lovely! Did you pick this out yourself?"

"I want to take credit, but the lady at the boutique picked it out along with the shoes."

"Why don't you to go back inside and put it on? I think I figured out your dress size, but wasn't sure about your shoe size, so I bought a few different sizes; they're in the truck."

I look down at my dress, slightly unsure about what I chose, and immediately go to the truck and pick out my shoes.

"Jamie, our reservations aren't until seven o'clock, so don't worry about being late."

"You want me to go put this on now?" I finally manage to ask.

"Yes, it will look great against your skin and I didn't want you to feel uncomfortable or out of place, so I bought it for you." I nod slowly and start to walk back to the house. "Oh," he says, "don't forget the shoes just grab your size."

I turn back and grab a size eight out of the trunk. "Okay, I'll go slip this on. I'll be right back." I walk back up to the front door and holler as I rush to my room. "It's just me, Mama!"

She pokes her head into the main hall, "Why? I thought you were leaving?"

"We are, but Daniel bought me this beautiful dress and shoes to wear out tonight."

"What was wrong with what you had on?"

"Nothing, he just asked me to wear this; apparently, it's more appropriate for where we're going." I step out of my room wearing the new dress and fitting my feet into my heels. I'm so glad the earrings and purse I bought match perfectly. "How does it look, Mama? Please, don't say anything negative. He didn't have to buy it, so I'm grateful for the thought."

"You looked beautiful before and you look just as beautiful now. Just be careful and take your time with him, Jamie."

"Mama, come on. Not now, please. I hope you and Steve have a nice date tonight. Go get dressed and have fun." Mama nods, puckering her lips. I make my way back toward the front door. "I'll see you later, Mama!" I say before I shut the door behind myself.

Daniel leans against the passenger side door, waiting for me. "Well, it's about time, pretty lady. You look amazing! I'm glad everything fits."

"Thank you so much for everything, Daniel. I love this dress and the shoes."

"Good. Now, let's get going. We should be right on time for our reservations."

He helps me into the car and gently shuts the door for me. I can't believe he wants me. Who is this man? I don't have anything to offer him. And who is Mama to criticize him? She didn't think twice about moving in a stranger with us. Just because she'd known him for a while didn't mean anything to Kelsie and me. Then, she makes all these little comments about Daniel. It's not like she's a great judge of character—just look at Steve. I think I'm a little better at judging people than she is. Daniel's never been anything but perfectly kind and gentlemanly toward me.

∞∞∞∞

I slam my hand down on my alarm as it goes off again after I hit snooze for the second time. I need to get up and get to class. I had a hard time getting up for Sunday morning service yesterday too; I had Mama drop me off because I needed to sleep in. Daniel and I had been out quite late on Saturday. Once again, it was amazing. I sigh and burrow deeper into my pillows. I can't make myself get out of bed. Daniel showers me with gifts and attention; I love it. He's incredible and a great kisser. But what do I know? I don't have anyone one to compare him to. He's intense and very romantic. He seems so patient, not like I'd imagine a man with his experience would be.

I can't stop thinking about the way he kissed me Saturday night. It wasn't like the other times before—it had been more than just a quick peck or polite press of lips. It was a deep, passionate kiss. It felt kind of like a training session for me at first—I'd never been kissed like that and I didn't know how. I caught on with ease, thankfully, as it quickly became intense. My whole body came alive under his kisses. I've never felt that way before. I felt areas of my body light up in ways I can't explain. I hope he's my first in every way, but we're going slowly; he says he's taking his time with me.

I think that's good? I'm not sure what to do, or if he thinks I'm just not experienced enough to go any faster. I mean, I'm not, but I can learn. I want him to know I can handle it. I'm an adult. Oh, who am I fooling? I don't know anything about that stuff except what Kelsie's told me, things Mama let drop in her conversations, and TV and movies of course. Lord knows the things they do on TV seem so unreal. I can't imagine making love.

I manage to get out of bed and into the shower. I'm meeting up with Daniel after class today. He says he'll be waiting right outside the building where I have my last class, just like the gentlemen he is. I can't seem to relax enough to eat properly around him yet. He makes me feel weak at the knees and so nervous. Kelsie doesn't understand why I'm so head-over-heels for him. I've tried explaining how amazing and generous he is. He's nothing like the guys I go to college with or those we were around growing up. He makes me feel like a woman; he understands where I want to be in life. Kelsie thinks I'm moving too fast, though she doesn't know we've only kissed. She thinks I'm too inexperienced for someone like him. I'm going to show both her and Mama that I can handle myself. I'm a grown woman whether they want to face that fact or not. Inexperienced doesn't mean stupid.

Daniel and I have been dating for a while now and he seems to be introducing me more and more into his world. He knows a lot of very important people. He has more money than I originally thought. Nothing ever seems to prevent him from getting what he wants, whether it's reservations at a restaurant or a suit tailored before a meeting. I'm not sure what kind of business he does, but it requires him to attend a lot of meetings, dinner parties, and out-of-town appointments. I like learning more about him. Little by little, I've met a few more of his acquaintances. The men I meet always look at me first before turning to Daniel and saying something like, "She's a keeper, Danny-boy." I like the admiration. I feel good inside and it makes me feel like I belong. Maybe I am good enough for him. His friends have all been lovely and kind and they all seem to think I'm worthy of him, or at least no one's said otherwise. Besides, he needs me; he says it all the time.

Chapter Eight

February 1992

 I wonder how Jace is doing and whether the community outreach is going well. I haven't seen or talked with him since the Christmas outreach event. He took me home that evening and we spent at least two hours talking outside my house. He's such a nice, caring guy. He listens to me ramble on and never interrupts me. I bet he learned how to listen when he became a minister. He has to listen to the whole congregation and help everyone. He checks on me, all the time. Mama says he calls at least once a week. I haven't had time to call him back lately. I'm a horrible volunteer and a worse friend. I do consider him a good friend, but I wish I were a better one to him. When we see each other, it's as if there's only the two of us are in the room. I think some people are just connected on some level like that. We can talk and laugh for hours without running out of things to say or feeling awkward. He gives me good advice. He's such a giving person. If Daddy were still alive, he'd tell me to marry a guy like Jace, someone who's grounded in his faith and puts the needs of others before his own. But, I still don't think of Jace that way. It would dishonor what I have and feel for Daniel.

I've been up since 4 a.m. I woke up and haven't been able to go back to sleep. I swear someone was watching me while I slept. I woke up and it felt like there was someone's warm breath on my face. I know I wasn't dreaming when I felt it. I had been sleeping, but drifting in that place where you're somewhat awake too. The only person here who walks around at night in the dark is Steve. I don't know what he was doing in my room, but I'm locking my door every night from now on. I stopped not too long ago; I let my guard down, but never again. I won't sleep another day in this house with him lurking around here watching and stalking me in secret. That man is purposely trying to run me away from here. I know he's not interested in me; he just wants to scare me away.

At lunch the other day, I told Daniel how I feel about Steve. I mentioned wanting to get a job and saving up so I can move closer to campus. He told me not to worry about it, that he'd handle it. I don't know about that. I don't want him handling everything for me. I won't wait very long either because I don't trust Steve. He's very obvious in his hate for me. I think I'm going to apply for some jobs this afternoon. Daniel said he had a big surprise coming for me and to trust him to work things out. He wants me to lean on him completely. I don't know if that's good or bad. Mama did with Daddy—she allowed him to lead her—but Daniel and I aren't married or even engaged.

∞∞∞∞

I haven't heard from Daniel in a few days. This is so unlike him. We went on a boat ride near Lake Jackson the last time I saw him. The boat was medium sized—just right for us. He named it Dark Shadow. Daniel has his own sailboat and he drove it like a pro. We could see the stars so clear and I didn't mind a bit that is was freezing cold. It was just the water, the chilly wind, and us. Even though the cold seemed unbearable, we managed to have so much fun. He's so romantic. I told Kelsie and she was speechless, maybe because her little sister is living in Texas like a queen. She still acts like I'm the same inexperienced girl she left, but I've changed in so many ways over the past two years. Life so far has been my teacher. I'm different now that I'm with Daniel. I see life differently. I'm ready to live, just like she was when she left.

I pick up the phone and dial Daniel's phone. A strange voice picks up, a man, but definitely not Daniel.

"Hello, I'm sorry, I might have misdialed. May I please speak with Daniel?"

"This is Daniel's phone, but he isn't available. Is this Jamie?"

I smile. Whoever this was knows who I am. "Yes, I'm just trying to get a hold of him."

"Hi Jamie, this is Mylow. I'm Daniel's friend."

"Oh, of course. I remember you from the dinner party. It's been a few days since I spoke with him. Is he okay?"

"Yes, Ms. Jamie. He's out of town on important business. I'll let him know you called."

He just up and left? "Do you know when he'll be back?"

"In a few days or so."

"Okay, thanks Mylow." I hang up, more confused than ever. Why is his friend answering his phone? And why didn't he tell me he was leaving town? I'm missing him like crazy. Maybe it was an emergency business trip and he didn't have the time. But, he could have called from his hotel, surely. I need to find something to do; I don't want to seem desperate. I was productive last night at least. I spent all night writing a poem for Jace.

I know what I must do. I'll go to the church and apologize to Jace in person. I should have done this a long time ago. I was wrong for not returning his calls and for not focusing on the volunteering duties I signed up for. He is such a great person, and he helps so many people. Maybe he'll need my help today. I can't believe how I've acted. I only show up when it's convenient for me and that's not right. I like being there though; I like helping, I just get so caught up in Daniel. I'm all over the place right now. I've never been so disoriented before. The last time I saw Jace he was so overwhelmed, but he is strong and determined. I hope his stress has eased. He's the most caring guy I know. He always put others first, all the time. And then look at me! I know better. I take his kindness for granted too. I guess I could keep in touch and check on him sometimes. I owe him a sincere apology, but I haven't managed it yet. So, I hope he likes the poem I wrote him. It's my way of giving back to him. I better get out of here if I don't want to be here when Steve gets home. I'll take the bus since I don't have class tomorrow and it won't matter what time I get home.

The church is emptier than it usually is, which I guess makes sense since it's the evening. I look around for Jace, but he spots me first.

"Hello Ms. Moore, how are you?"

"Good, and you?"

"I'm well, glory be to God, thank you for asking. How is your mother?"

"She's as good as can be, and better than she has been in a long while."

"And your sister?" I'm touched he remembers to ask about everyone in my family.

"Kelsie is doing well. She's trying to run my life from California, but that's what big sisters do, right?"

"Just think, she knows you better than anyone else. She just wants to make sure you're doing okay back home."

"Oh, I know, but she still thinks of me as a baby, not a grown woman."

"It's really good to see you. Is everything okay?"

"Yes, everything is fine. I hope this is a good time. I know I popped in unannounced."

"Now is fine, Ms. Moore."

"Great," I smile at him, relieved. "I came by because I wanted to apologize in person for the times I have stood you up and for not returning your phone calls. My actions are unacceptable. I'm not cut out for this, I guess."

"No, don't say that."

"I know you were counting on me, and it was wrong of me to behave that way. So, I want to say I'm sorry."

"You didn't have to come all the way down here to say that. A phone call would have been good enough. I figured you had a lot going on with school. God's promises and word never return void. We had enough help. While we've missed your presence, we made due and there will be more opportunities. This is a lifestyle, Ms. Moore."

"Yes, it is. Let me get to the other reason I came all the way here on the bus."

"You are some lady, Ms. Moore. Now that you're here, can you stay awhile? If not, I understand."

"Yes, but I have to make sure I can catch the bus before it's too late."

Loneliness Within

"Are you sure you want to catch the bus this late? If you can stay for a little while, I can wrap up these last few things and take you home," he asks.

"Oh, before I forget, I have something for you. I wrote this myself and I want you to have it. It's nothing special, but it's yours if you want it."

"Wow, you wrote this and you're giving it to me? What did I do to deserve this?"

"You give to so many people—the church, the youth, the outreach ministry—and I wanted to give you something for a change. Plus, it was weighing on my heart and I wanted you to forgive me. I want to give back to you."

"All I ask, Ms. Moore, is that you read the words aloud just the way you meant for me to hear them. Please? I promise I'll never forget it."

"Okay, I will. The poem is called 'Man of Purpose.'"

A free spirited man,
Possessing great diligence.
The gentle man,
With desires that know no limits.
Striving for excellence,
He endures.
Loving, strong, full of life
Never timid,
A man sure of himself and what he wants,
He goes after it.

85

Assertive and independent,
That he is.
Without a negative word to say,
He forgives.
God's special gift,
Wrapped into his display,
Destiny lies in his hands,
He's not afraid to carry out the plan.
Not ashamed to shout,
Yes,
I have purpose,
Yes, I got the nerve.
Willing to walk through life's trials,
Watching them whither and burn.
A man with class,
I've had his experience,
Surely a tough act to follow.
A leader that cares,
Respects and upholds dignity,
I'm down with you,
I'm proud of you,
Because you are without a doubt
A strong man,
Determined to fulfill your purpose.

Jace takes a moment to read over the poem while I recite it aloud by memory. His expression shifts to one of sincere gratitude.

"That was deep. You've really surprised me this evening. You have a gift, Ms. Jamie. Do you write often?"

"Sometimes, but for fun mostly. When I'm bored, it keeps me out of trouble. I mostly write about things close to my heart." Jace looks away from me, his eyebrows knitting together tightly. "Oh, did I say something wrong? I'm sorry."

"No, you are full of surprises, Jamie. How could anyone ever peel back all the wonderful layers God has placed inside of you?"

"I've said it before but you sound like my dad. He was a wise man like you." The clock chimes 7 p.m.

Jace startles slightly. "Oh, I've lost track of the time. I have to get these boxes of food packed for tomorrow."

"I'll help you."

"Thank you, Jamie. Not just for helping me, but also for giving me so much more—a mental break, something I dearly needed. You are so refreshing." I felt a blush overtake my cheeks.

"Jace, you're welcome, but you must know how you inspire and motivate me. You make me want to do more for myself and others."

We share a grin and then get to work packing the food donation boxes for the soup kitchen.

Later, as we pull into my driveway, Jace turns to me and sincerely says, "Jamie, before you get out the car, I want to say thank you again. Anytime you want to drop by the church, please do. You helped so much tonight. I would not have been able to get those meals packed without you."

"It was my pleasure. You're excellent company."

"Maybe next time I can come by and pick you up so you don't have to ride the bus."

"Oh, yeah, that would be so helpful, but soon I hope to move closer to the school so I won't have to ride it as much." I pause with my hand on the door handle. "It's just not working out here with my mom's boyfriend living with us. We don't get along, and, well, I'll just say he's not to be trusted. As soon as I have the opportunity to move I'll be taking it."

"I'm glad you're looking out for yourself, Jamie. Be sure to pray for God to lead you where he wants you to go. Ask him for peace, clarity, and strength. He will give it to you; he always listens."

"You are so special, Reverend Jace Lawrence. You will make some woman really happy one day."

"Jamie, can I pray with you?"

"Yes, that would be very nice." Jace takes my hand in his as we bow our heads.

"Father God, I'm coming to you this blessed night with Ms. Jamie Moore. She's dealing with life-altering choices. If she should face challenges along her journey, strengthen her for the battles to come. Father, give her peace in her spirit and mind. Help her to know there is no failure if she walks with you. Let not her heart be troubled but full of love and peace. Bestow grace and mercy upon her life and those of her family. I pray for the total restoration for her mother. In Jesus' name, amen."

"Amen. Thank you, Jace. That meant the world to me." I lean forward and quickly kiss his cheek before exiting the car. I walk up to the door and wave to Jace as he waits for me to get inside safely.

"Mama, it's me! Don't worry, I'm going straight to bed."

"Jamie?"

"Yes, you didn't have to get up. I'm just coming in."

"I wanted to tell you that man has been calling for you."

"Daniel?"

"Yes, he called a couple of times asking questions. I don't like it. I told him just try calling back tomorrow because you were out."

"He was probably worried about me. It's late and he knows I don't have a car to get around this time of night. I'll call him back. Thank you and goodnight, Mama."

I quickly dial Daniel's number and his answering machine picks up. "Hi Daniel, when you get my message please call me back. I'm home now. Talk to you later."

The days wear on. First, I don't hear from Daniel for one week, then two. Now, it's been three entire weeks since we last spoke. He's not answering and he's not returning my calls. I don't know what to think. Maybe he's moved on and wants nothing to do with me. I should have been here when he called. Why did I have to go to the church that night? I've probably messed everything up with him. I just can't figure him out, though. He disappeared on me first. I called and called him. Then, out of the blue, he calls back and I wasn't at home to answer. If he's upset about my missing one evening of his calls, then I should be furious with how little regard he's given my efforts to talk to him. And, what does he do after he can't get a hold of me? He disappears again. I have to stop thinking about this. But I keep wondering if he's in trouble or maybe even sick. I can't stand to think about that; I care too much about him.

No, I have to stop this madness. I need to focus on school. I'm stopping by the financial aid office today to see if I can work on campus to earn money. I need to prepare to move out. I'm not coming back tonight until I've found an apartment. I don't have a dime to pay for it right now, but I will. I'm getting out of here. I must step out on faith and believe things will work out. Maybe Daniel will take me more seriously if I'm not living at home. I'll show him I'm woman who can handle a man like him. I know he may think my mom is a bit over protective of me, but he doesn't know I've never dated before and she's just worried.

Loneliness Within

∞∞∞

April 1992

I'm almost shaking with excitement. The financial aid office gave me such amazing news. I not only qualify for work-study, but I can get a job on campus right away. They also told me I qualify for a merit scholarship based on my grades last semester. Not only can I move, but I can get a place with furniture included! Daddy would be so proud of me and I bet Daniel will be too. I know he may never call me again, but with my good luck today, I think I'll try to call him one more time. If he doesn't answer, I'll know we're finished and I'll force myself to let go.

Spring is all about new beginnings. Winter has faded and I can feel the season changing and warming up. The flowers are blooming and the breeze is warm and feels good brushing across my skin. I stop into the cafe on campus and ordered my favorite bagel with strawberry cream cheese to go. When she brings it to me, I ask to use the phone for a quick call. I fold the bag tightly as she waves me over to the phone at the host's stand. I dial Daniel's number one last time and wait for the machine.

"Hello?" Oh! He picked up!

"Daniel? Thank God! Are you okay? I've been worried sick. I've been calling you."

"Yeah, I noticed, but like I told you when we started dating, I need you to be available when I need you. That's important to me."

"Yes, you did say that, but I waited and waited for you to return my call. And you never did. Then, the one night that I'm out—"

"Jamie, shh. Listen to me. Hang up the phone and come outside." The phone clicks in my ear; he hung up. I stare at the phone for a moment unable to believe he hung up on me. I think back over what he just said. Is he outside? How would he know where I am? I look out the big picture window at the front of the cafe and there he is.

I rush out the door, my bagel forgotten on the counter. "Daniel, what are you doing out here?"

"I was waiting to see you."

"Why didn't you say that on the phone?"

"I wanted to surprise you."

"I didn't recognize this car. It's a different one. Where have you been?" I ask emotionally.

"Hey, it's okay. Just stop, breathe, and listen to me. I never want to call you or depend on you only to find you're not there for me. When you weren't there, I realized maybe you needed some time to think about things and figure out your priorities."

"I didn't need time away from you. I missed you so much!"

"I bet you did."

"I was so worried. All I could think about was whether I'd ever see you again."

"Get in the car, pretty lady."

I climbed in. "Daniel, please don't do this to me again."

"I have a surprise for you this weekend. Can you get away for a few days?"

"Of course, I can. Where are we going? Can I have a hint so I know what to bring?"

"Just bring a small bag. I'll provide everything you'll need."

"Daniel, you mean so much to me. I don't know what I would do if I lost you. You have me, I promise. I'll always be where you need me to be."

"I'm holding you to that, Jamie. Don't let this happen again."

Daniel puts on his seatbelt and starts the car. "I guess the real question is what your mama's going to say. I don't think she'd agree to her baby staying out for the whole weekend."

"Daniel, I'm a grown woman, not a baby. I can do what I please. Don't worry about that. I'll be ready when you pick me up." We talk until his phone rings. He answers, talks a bit, and hangs up before apologizing for the interruption.

"I'll be by Friday around 3 p.m. I'm looking forward to spending this weekend with you, Jamie." We pull into my driveway and he slides the car into park. "Well, baby, you're home. I must go, but I'll see you Friday." He leans over to kiss me.

"Thanks for the ride home."

"No need to thank me." He kisses my lips again and says, "This is what I do for my lady." I climb out of the car and wave as he leaves before I walk up to the front door.

Once inside, I turn and lean back against the door and let out a little squeal. Oh my God! He has asked me over for the weekend! I'm assuming I'll finally get to see his house. I've been waiting seven months for this. Wow! I can't believe we've been together so long, and he's been so patient to take it this slowly for me. I'm so in love, but I'm definitely too afraid to say it. I didn't think I'd ever see him again. Then, not only do I see him again, but also he was waiting for me so he could surprise me! Why was I so worried? He wouldn't just disappear and leave me high and dry. I can't believe this! I want to call Kelsie and tell her everything, but I'm afraid she won't understand. Oh, it doesn't matter. I need tell someone. I'm bursting with excitement! I grab the phone and call her, but I get her machine.

After the beep, I leave a message, "Kelsie, please call me back as soon as you can. I have something to tell you. I'm so excited! Love you, sis. Bye!" I hang up and head to the shower.

Kelsie's probably out with her boyfriend. She's been so happy with him. She's so much more content than I've ever known her to be. I think I know a little bit about how that feels. Daniel makes me happy. He really makes me feel like I'm a part of something.

Mama can't seem to understand, though. She thinks it's crazy that he's never taken me to visit his home. She keeps telling me he's married and cheating on his wife. She thinks she has it all figured out. When I tell her I'm spending the weekend with him at his house, she's going to be so shocked. I hope Kelsie calls back soon; I want to share my news.

I couldn't sleep last night just thinking about this weekend and wondering if Daniel will want to do more than just kiss me. I can handle him; I'm a grown woman. I want him to know that. I have to show him I'm not afraid. I want to be everything he needs. I'm a little nervous, but I guess this is how it goes. It's not like I can ask anyone. I'll have to learn on my own. I keep daydreaming about us finally being together. I want him to teach me how to please him.

After class, I manage to catch Mama before Steve gets home. I knock on her bedroom door, where I can hear her humming. She's probably in here sewing. I sure hate to intrude on her happy parade.

"Mama, are you in there?" I call through the door.

"Yes, honey. Come in."

"No, thanks. I'll wait for you to come out here."

"Jamie, just come in, please. I'm in the middle of something."

"No, ma'am, I can wait." I can't help but stand firm on this. There's just no way I'm going into my daddy's room—the room she's now sharing with that sick man. It disgusts me in every way. He doesn't have any respect for her or me. When he uses the restroom, he leaves the door open—even when I'm walking right by! No, thank you, I'll avoid any further disgust at all costs.

I hear my mama huff and set something on the ground before coming to the door and opening it. "Yes, Jamie, what is it?"

"Mama, I want to you know I'll be going to Daniel's house for the weekend. He invited me over and I don't have too much studying to do this week, so I said I'd go. I thought I should tell you so you didn't worry when I didn't come home."

"So, you're going for the whole weekend?"

96

"Yes, ma'am. It's about time I start living my life. I—" the words catch in my throat. I clear my throat and try again. "I also wanted to tell you that I'm moving out soon. I'm starting a job on campus and that combined with my financial aid is enough to pay for an apartment near campus."

Mama's face pinched together tightly, like she was sucking on a lemon.

"Mama, aren't you happy for me?" She doesn't say anything—just stands there, waiting for me to continue. "The truth is you've been so strong and happy for a while now. Steve makes you happy and he'd love to have you all to himself. I'm in the way and that's not fair to either of us. I have to live my life too. You'll be fine. I'll visit as much as you want me to." She just keeps staring at me, waiting for something, but I don't know what. "Don't look like that, Mama. Please say something."

She shakes her head silently and turns around, gently closing the door behind her and leaving me in the hall. "Please don't do this. Please just say something. Mama?"

Chapter Nine

I'm leaving to spend the weekend with Daniel today and Mama hasn't said a word, at least not to me, since I told her the news. She's really upset and I'm not even sure why. I don't know if it's because I'm leaving for the weekend or because I'm moving out, or both. I hope she'll understand when she's back to her normal self. Once she is, and I think she can handle it, I'll tell her just how mean and hateful Steve has been to Kelsie and me. Every time I try to tell her now, I look in her eyes and remember how depressed she was when Daddy died. I won't send her back to that state of mind. She would blame herself and that's more sadness piling on top of her progress. I'll just kept my mouth shut instead and let him take care of her like he desperately wants. I think he wishes she didn't have children; he wants her all to himself. I just want her to be happy and not have to work so hard to get by. He provides for her well enough and that's what she needs right now.

Leaving this weekend is good. It will allow her time to process everything I said. At least, that's what I tell myself. I need to stop over thinking this and focus on spending the weekend with my man. He'll be here to pick me up soon. I have a small bag packed, just like he said I should. I can't wait until I see what he has planned for us. I walk down to the living room, bag in hand, and see Mama sitting in her chair by the big window.

"Mama," I say, "I'll be leaving soon. I just want you to know I put Daniel's number and full name in the kitchen drawer, so you'll have it in an emergency."

Mama barely nods. I wonder if she's even listening.

"I also wrote down his license plate number, just in case I don't return the police will know where to find me. Just kidding! Is there anything else I forgot to do?"

She doesn't say a word in response. I sigh. The side door off the kitchen slams shut. "Please don't sit there and ignore me. I'm standing right here talking to you."

"Damn, you and your sister are selfish. Neither of you care about your mama at all," Steve says as he walks in from the kitchen.

"Excuse me? How dare you say that to me? I love my mama with everything I have in me. Before you came here, we were all very close. We have done everything we could for Mama and for each other. We're a family. How could you say that?" I turn toward my mother. "Mama, don't listen to him. Kelsie and I love you and you know it." She still doesn't respond and my heart breaks a little. "Look, I've tried to respect you, Steve, but enough is enough. I ask that you never speak to me or disrespect me in that manner again."

"I'll say whatever the hell I want. If you don't like it, you can get out."

"Get out? Get out of where, Steve? This is my daddy's house. He worked himself to death to pay for this house. If you think you can kick me out of his house, you're wrong. You don't own a thing in here. None of this is yours—this is my mama's, Kelsie's, and mine. How dare you try to put me out of something you don't own?"

"That's enough, Jamie! You will not talk to Steve that way. He's only looking out for my best interests."

"That's my point exactly, Mama!"

"Nobody will be getting put out of here today," she says firmly, wiping her hands across her face. "I'm tired right now. I'm going to my bedroom to lie down."

"Mama, are you okay? I never wanted to upset you. I'm sorry for getting into it with him. I know me leaving and moving on my own is better for everyone. We'll fight less." I kiss her on her cheek before she heads in her room. I hear Daniel's car turn into the driveway. "Daniel's here. I'm leaving. I'll lock up behind myself and call you later."

Mama nods and makes her way carefully to her bedroom.

I pick up my bag and unlock the front door, but before I can leave, Steve grabs my arm. He pulls me close and I try to pull away from his grip, but not before he can whisper, "Jamie, do us all a favor and learn to please that man so he can help you get the hell out of here. Learn some tricks, keep your big mouth shut, and maybe then he'll keep you."

"Go to hell, Steve," I snarl as I slam the door behind myself. As I lock it, I can hear him laughing through the thick, old wooden door. Daniel's only halfway up the walk by the time I'm off the porch.

"Hey, beautiful lady, couldn't wait—what's wrong?" he asks. I shrug.

"Nothing, I'm just ready to leave now. There's no need to come inside. My mama's sleeping and doesn't feel well."

"Okay, if you say so," he says, taking my bag and leading me back to his car. He shuts the door behind me and then climbs in on his side.

I watch the scenery from the window. The houses in our neighborhood aren't what they use to be and the people who live in them are strangers now. I wish I never had to go back home again. I can't keep it inside anymore. Daniel, as if sensing my tension, puts his hand on my knee as he drives.

"I hate that man so much. He loves to make me miserable. He enjoys it."

"I know, baby. I'm sorry you have to deal with him."

"Daniel, you don't understand. He's two different people: one person in front of my mama and a demon when she's not around."

"Is he really that bad?"

"She doesn't have a clue about who he really is. The saddest part is that he's so in love with her. It's sickening. He would do anything to keep her happy, but can't bear sharing her. He'd love to stuff me in a closet and starve me to death if he could."

"Jamie, stop! Maybe he loves your mom and you two just don't get along, but no one is perfect. Everyone has things about them others may not agree with. He wants her all to himself; I can respect that. He feels that you're grown and you should be out on your own as well."

"Yeah, but he was the same way before I was grown, when he first moved in. But, you're right; it's time for me to move out and on my own. There is something I want to tell you."

"Okay, but first I have a surprise for you. It may be the answer to all of your problems. I've been working on this for a while now. It took a lot to make this happen, more time than I anticipated, and I'm hoping you'll want to be a part of it."

"What is it? Daniel, you've already done so much for me. You didn't have to get me anything."

"Well, this is a little different than just a gift."

"I don't know what to say. You're so generous and giving. I feel so honored and unworthy all at the same time. How can I ever repay you for all the things you've done?"

"You'll have plenty of time for that."

"So, where are we going?"

"It's a surprise—all of this is a surprise. Just wait and see."

"I feel so free when I leave that house. Oh, and about what I wanted to tell you—" The car phone rings and interrupts me.

"Hold on, I've been waiting on this call and I have to take it." I nod and he picks it up.

He's unbelievable sometimes. I know he'll be proud to know I'm moving into my own place. When he gets off the phone, I'll tell him and ask if he wants to see apartments with me. I wonder what his big surprise is and why it took so long to finish. Daniel loves me. I know he does. There is no other explanation for all of this other than he really loves me. I have to make this work. I know he doesn't like for me to ask a lot of questions about his business life and stuff, so I won't ask. I don't need to know about his work. I'll be patient and let him guide me.

Daniel hangs up the phone. "Jamie, close your eyes."

"What?"

"Close your eyes. Trust me."

"Okay." He stops the car and comes around to open my door. "Open your eyes."

The house is two stories tall with a small waterfall in the front yard. The entry has large, dark wood, double doors. Seeing all the windows and the sheer size of it, I know this house must have at least five or six bedrooms.

"Is this where you live?"

"Yes, do you like it?"

"Like it?

"Do I like it? Of course I do. I've never seen the inside of a house this big and beautiful before in my life. This is where you live? You must be appalled to come to our neighborhood, and oh my goodness, my house. I'm so embarrassed even more now."

"No, I would never say anything like that about your house. I'll go anywhere for you. Don't you ever forget that! Come in. Let me show you around. I want you to feel comfortable with every single room in this place."

"This is the most beautiful house I've ever seen. You've lived here all this time?"

"Yes and no. I live here and at my condo. I've been working on the house for a while, but it was always missing something important. Let's go upstairs." We walk up the grand staircase and into the central hallway. He leads me to a doorway, but stops me from entering.

"Jamie, hold on. Before we go into this room, well, it's special to me. I hope it will be to you too. Now go on in."

I open the door and I am stunned. "Oh wow! This is your bedroom? Look at the mirror—it's huge! And your bed, can I touch it? It looks like I would melt inside of it."

"Yes, but we need to talk." He walks over and sits on a small loveseat.

"Your bedroom has its own small living area with a fireplace!"

"Come sit down with me. I know we've been seeing each other for a while. At least, it seems that way to me."

"Daniel, we've been seeing each other for seven months, one week, and one day."

"Well, I know you hate being at your mom's house with her boyfriend. Plus, let's face it, you're taking the bus and walking everywhere you go. I've been working over the last few weeks trying to get this house ready so you couldn't resist it."

"What do you mean? No one could resist wanting to live in a house like this."

"I want you to live in this house...with me."

"What?"

"I want you to wake up here every day. I have a complicated and dangerous life. I've never told you that before. I couldn't because I didn't think you were ready to know. As you see, I know a lot of people, but with friends come enemies. I provide an important service to very powerful people and your safety and their privacy are my top priorities. But you have to understand that if you say yes and come here, you will never be able to return to your mother's house, at least not for a while. Life as you know it will be over."

"Wait, what? Daniel I can't just leave my mother and never return. I need to see her."

"Jamie, your mom will be well-taken care of by Steve. I'm not saying you can't check on her—not at all. I'll make sure she's provided for financially. Going back to the house will be out of the question for now, but we can discuss it more later. This is a commitment and it must be something you want to do." I was so nervous. Why wouldn't he let me go back to my daddy's house? I grew up there. It meant so much to me. "Sometimes, pretty lady, a good life comes with a price. I know it's a lot to think about. Make the best decision for you. If you want to be here with me, I'll have you."

"Daniel, of course I want to be with you. But what would I do about school? How will I get there from all the way out here?"

"College is almost out for the summer right?"

"Yes, just another couple of weeks."

"Then we can work something out before next semester. Think about it before you agree, but don't take too long. I'm not a patient man. Now, why don't you go see the bathroom and closet, and tell me what you think?"

"Daniel!" I scream happily. "Oh! This closet is amazing! But there are clothes and shoes in here already. Whose things are these?" I ask, holding out a lovely woman's dress.

"Pretty lady, all those things belong to you."

"What?" This has to be a dream. No one just bumps into someone like him ends up with all of this. Is this is too good to be true? I'm sure Cinderella didn't feel this good. "Daniel, you are too much!"

"Jamie, look in the closet and pick out a dress. We have a very special dinner date tonight. Try out the shower and get ready. I have to run out for a little while, but I'll meet you downstairs in an hour, please be ready." I quickly hug him and then run back into the closet to choose a dress.

I pick the first one that stands out. It's a soft blue with a ribbon around the waist. I take my time and decide to head straight for the big oval tub. It's big enough for my legs to actually stretch out and float. After a while, I pry myself out of the water and finally get my hair and makeup perfect. I'm downstairs in just shy of two hours. I sit down in the living room to wait for him, wondering how he had the wall art placed so flawlessly and where he bought such beautiful paintings from. Everything in this house looks expensive.

∞∞∞

It's been almost three hours and he's not back yet. I'm beyond worried. I explored the house, trying to find him—or, well, anyone. I found Mylow, but he couldn't tell me anything. I walk upstairs to the master bath to touch up my makeup again when I hear him.

"Jamie? Jamie!"

"Yes?"

"Are you in there?"

"Yes. Give me a minute, please."

"Woman, I gave you a few hours."

I finish touching up my lipstick and smooth my hair back to perfection before opening the door. "What's wrong? Are you okay? Why do you look so upset?"

"I just had something go terribly wrong at exactly the wrong time. I was caught up with business and I had every intention on coming back a long time ago. I'm sorry. I promise I'll make it up to you. Sadly, this is my life, Jamie. People can really piss me off and it can go wrong really fast. I need to know if you're with me. It's complicated and risky. I'm not like a normal guy. I don't sit in an office every day and work behind a desk." He takes my hand in his and holds it tightly. "If you want to be with me, you must be all in. There is no going back if you choose to be here. You can't. I won't let you. It compromises my life and my business. I have friends and enemies everywhere."

"Daniel, I want to be with you. I don't care about how long it took you to get back tonight. You're here now. How do I look?" I ask as I spin for him.

"You look...you look amazing, especially with your hair up like that."

"I know you like my hair up for special dates. I'm learning, right?"

"Yes, you are and you're doing one hell of a job. We have some incredible plans tonight, beautiful. We're somewhat delayed, but it'll work. Tonight, you'll meet some of my VIP acquaintances—I have never had anyone else around them. You will be the first woman they've seen me with me. Are you ready?" I nod and he leads me out to the car.

"I want to prepare you for the dinner guests we're accompanying tonight. They're very powerful people. I'll order for you, so don't be nervous about the food either. I want you to feel comfortable. They'll know if you don't belong. I've told them a little about you, but they're not aware of where you live or where you're from, which is good. Try not to talk much about your home life. Just leave the conversations up to me. I know you'll do great."

"You're acting like this is an interview or something."

"It is like that in some ways, but not the kind of interview you're thinking of. You have to help me tonight. I need you. Just relax, let me lead, and don't worry—just stay beautiful." We pull into a small, private parking lot for valet. "Before we go in I want to tell you something. I can't really think of anyone else at this moment who I would rather have with me."

"I appreciate that. Thank you, and don't worry. Everything will be fine."

"The people we're meeting tonight are really important to me and to my business. I must make a good impression. We're together, so have some fun and just be you. I have something else planned for us when we're done with dinner. Let's nail this."

"Whatever I can do to help I will."

"That's why I like you, Jamie. You center me. I need you to stay just like this. Don't change on me, ever."

"I won't."

∞∞∞

Daniel's a natural charmer. He's dazzling the entire table. His confidence seems effortless. He looks over at me and winks. I guess that's his way of saying I'm doing great. I don't have anything to say really. I don't understand their world or the business conversation they're having. They're speaking over me on purpose, I believe. I'm not sure why or maybe it's just me. Their conversations are so uninteresting that eventually I tune them out. I'm on autopilot, like a scientist watching subjects through a glass window.

The music playing from the live jazz band is familiar; it reminds me of the music Mr. Jackson would play in his car when he visited Daddy. This song is "Masquerade". The words are telling I never really listened to them until now. *Lost in a masquerade*—the words might have expressed what Mr. Jackson was feeling at the time, now that I think about it. Life can be confusing. I would hate to live a life behind a mask one face on the outside, but another person on the inside. What a sad and troubling way of being. I remember him saying that George Benson had a rare sound and spoke to the heart of things, most of his music made people feel good. I can't help but soak the entire experience in one moment at a time. This night is full of fine dining great music and people who carryon like they don't have a care in the world. The five-course meal is excellent. The chandeliers are breathtaking. I heard the lady next to me say they're made from real crystals. I'm pretty sure the cost of the food ordered at this table could feed a lot of hungry people. My leg bounces under the table, hidden by the draped white cloth. I decline wine and choose water from a fancy glass when offered. I didn't want to make a fool out of myself and I've never really had a drink before. Even though the food is delicious, I haven't eaten much of it. I'm just too nervous to eat like I really want to. I hope my nerves aren't obvious to everyone at the table. I know I'm one of the youngest women here. They've all been very nice. I hope everything works out for Daniel.

Thankfully, the dinner ended well. Daniel's overjoyed by the time they pull the car around. He opens the door for me and when he climbs in on his side, he can't help smiling.

"You did great, Jamie! I couldn't have asked for a better night. You deserve all of me tonight. I can't wait to get you home." All of him? What does that mean? Suddenly, my heart begins to race. It must show on my face because he asks, "Why do you look so startled?"

"Who me? No reason."

"I thought you would be happy."

"I am. I am happy."

"This was so important, and now it's over. I've sealed the deal. I can move past this thanks to you. Life is good. I want to focus the rest of this night on you."

Is he going to make love to me when we get back to the house? Could this be my chance to prove to him I'm woman enough?

"Jamie, you're quiet. Are you sure you're okay?"

"Yes, I'm fine. I can't wait to spend the rest of the weekend with you."

I'll be fine. I'm ready for this. Steve's words about keeping my mouth shut, learning some tricks, and being able to keep him ring in my head. I know this is going to work out. I know I'll be okay, but I'm so scared. I'm shaking. I don't even know for sure if he's planning something like that. My leg is bouncing up and down. I'm glad this dress makes it easy to hide.

We pull into his garage and I'm trying not to show him how nervous I am, but it has to be all over my face. I've got to get it together. He's going to think I'm just too inexperienced for a man like him.

"Jamie, I want you to go upstairs. There's something on the bed for you. Put it on."

"You're always surprising me," I say trying not to let my nerves creep into my voice.

"I'll be in after I shower." He winks and disappears into the bathroom.

I walk over to the bed and open a white box with a big lace bow. My goodness, look at this; it's beautiful. I think it's silk. I run to the bathroom to freshen up and try it on. This is what lingerie feels like! It contours to my body perfectly through my hips and then flows down to my ankles. The back drapes low, right above my waist. Wow, this is real. Tonight is going to happen. When did he have time to set this out? I've been waiting for him to connect with me for so long and now it's finally here. The man of my dreams is going to show me how to become a woman. I hope it's everything he wants it to be. Maybe then he'll truly love me like I love him.

"Come here, pretty lady. Let me see how you look." I spin for him in my negligée. "You look great. I take it you like what I left for you?"

"Yes, I do very much."

"Jamie, you're breathtaking. You make me a very happy man, especially tonight."

"How is that? I haven't done much but listen and follow your lead? I feel like I need to do more."

"Sit down, relax. Let's talk."

"You want me to talk?"

"No, Jamie, I want to talk. I know you have a lot of questions to ask me. Now is the time, so ask away."

"How old are you?"

"I'm 37." I hesitate before continuing on.

"Go on," he says. "I'm giving you the opportunity to ask me anything. I know you want to know more so ask."

"Since I get a free pass, I want to know more about your family, like your parents."

"What about them?"

"What kind of parents did you have growing up? Were they nice and easy going, or were they strict?"

"Well, they were a little bit of both, actually. I pretty much got my way with most things growing up. I was the only child. My father was a workaholic. He believed in hard work and providing for his family. He worked all the time. He was a simple man at heart, but his clothes—wow, the man could dress. When my father stepped out, he did it in style. He felt a man should smell and look good to keep his woman wanting more. He only had eyes for my mama; he was a faithful man."

"And your mom?"

"My mama was tough, like most women from her time. She had to be tough with me when I was young. She handled all the discipline, but loved hard. She was

115

wonderful, a really strong person. I had a decent life as a kid. I didn't see a lot of bad until I left their house. I always had a mind of my own and never wanted to follow the traditional way of living."

"What you mean?"

"I didn't want a little house, a regular job, a car, or a wife. That was one reason I decided to join the military. I felt it was important for me to live my own life my own way. I got into something my parents never liked. At the same time, I was able to live my life my way. I thought I had the best of both worlds. I had a hard time selling them on joining the military and that it was my road to success. And I was very successful at first, but it cost me a lot. You didn't ask about all of that; I'm rambling on."

"No, go on, this is good."

"I was just saying that it cost me a lot. I saw a lot of hell during my tours overseas. I saw so many bad things. My mama begged me to come home for good, but I decided to go back one last time. I was sent to Germany. Nine months later, I lost my mom. She had cervical cancer. She begged my father not to worry me about it. It hit her hard and fast. She was gone before I could return."

"Oh Daniel, I'm so sorry to hear it happened like that. I bet that was devastating."

"It was, but worse than that, just eighteen months later my dad died too. The doctor said he died from the grief of losing my mother, the only woman he ever loved.

They were so close. He couldn't live without her. When I got that call—the combination of losing the both of them broke me. I lost all sense of reality. I did things that left me in a dark place. A young man doing what his parents begged him not to do. I left them alone; I had to own that. They didn't care about my military success and medals. They wanted me home safe. Instead, I wanted my way. I still think I could have helped them more and made sure Mama went to the best doctors."

"Daniel, you must know that nothing you could have done would have changed their course and fate in life."

"I had to find some kind of understanding after Daddy died."

"I know that kind of pain."

"Yeah, the last two years I was in the military is a blank space for me. From time to time, I'm reminded of that person. I took away one thing from my tragedy and it was that I inherited everything they owned. But at the time, all I could focus on was the grief I still deal with to this day. I find myself working to numb it all. But enough of this sad talk, I hope I've answered a lot of your questions."

"There's just one more question."

"One more and that's it; we have plans."

"Have you ever been married or engaged?"

"No, not even close. Now, I need a drink."

"I've never seen you drink before."

"I do from time to time. You've also never known me to be so open about my past"

"True, it means a lot to me."

"Jamie, let's be clear. I don't ever want you messing with this stuff," he says gesturing to the bar, "I keep these shelves stocked with different bottles mostly for the art of collecting fine liquor from different places. I've seen what these bottles do to people. It will kill you from the inside out." I agreed and he took a deep breath, almost a sigh of relief. "Tonight Jamie, please don't allow me to sleep in bed with you. Before you think that I don't want to sleep in bed with you, it's not that at all. There're so many things that you don't know, so I'm asking you to trust me on this. Do not allow me to sleep in bed with you. If I fall asleep, wake me up right away. I need to sleep in the other room tonight. Can you do that for me?"

"Yes, of course, I can. I won't let you sleep next to me even though it's not what I want. I can't believe I'm here with you in this amazing house. I can't wrap my head around that you want to share this with me. I'm so emotional. I can't explain it—" He leans forward suddenly and cuts me off with a passionate kiss.

I can't believe this is happening. I feel things in places right now that I didn't even know existed. I want this man so bad.

"Daniel, I want you to know I've never been with a man."

"Shh, I know. Let me take care of you. Do you trust me?"

"Yes, I do."

"Then don't be afraid. Let me lead you."

Everything was amazing. I wake up slowly and stretch my pleasantly sore muscles carefully. As I move, I feel a heavy presence against my side and immediately open my eyes—no one should be here with me.

"Daniel," I say, surprised. "Daniel, wake up!" Oh God, he must be so tired. Why won't he wake up? What should I do? I guess I'll tell him in the morning that I tried.

The more I move, the more sore I feel. I slip out of bed and scramble into the bathroom, setting up a nice, hot bath. I love this bathroom. I climb into the tub and luxuriate in there, not having anyone lurking behind the door or watching through the cracks. I'm feeling deeply relaxed when a shout rings out from the bedroom. "Daniel, is that you? I tried waking you up." The shouting doesn't stop, so I climb out of the tub and hastily wrap a towel around my dripping wet self. I approach the bed cautiously and see Daniel writhing in the sheets.

"Wake up, Daniel. Wake up, it's a dream." I shake him, but he doesn't wake. "You're having a bad dream. Daniel! Please wake up!" Daniel startles awake and immediately sits up, breathing hard. "Are you okay? You're sweating. Do you need something to drink?" He doesn't respond. "What happened? I was in the tub—"

"Goddammit, Jamie! I told you not to let me fall asleep in here."

"I fell asleep with you. I woke up and remembered you didn't want to sleep in here, so I tried waking you up, but you wouldn't. I tried, Daniel. I promise I tried. I got up to take a bath and that's when I heard you yelling. I rushed right in here. I did everything but pour water on your face. I'm so sorry. Please don't be upset with me."

"I asked you to do this one thing for me!"

"I know, I'm sorry, Daniel. I didn't know that this would happen." He storms out of the room without looking back. I sit, stunned, on the bed, still damp from the tub. What just happened? I guess he had a nightmare—a really bad one—but I don't know what happened. I'm so lost. Why is he so upset over a nightmare? I've never seen anything like that before. I messed up, I guess. How could I do this to him? I failed him. I can only hope he forgives me.

∞∞∞

I hoped everything would be better in the morning, but it's not. I can't believe that such an amazing night ended so badly. I've never before felt the way I did last night. If I didn't want to admit how much I loved him before, I can't deny it now. My love for him is more than I can explain. I want to tell him. No, I am going to tell him. I hope he sees my heart and knows I'm sorry. I've looked for him everywhere: the garage, the backyard, and his office—he's gone. He left lunch already prepared for me on the counter, but I'm in this big house without him. Either he's still very upset or he had to leave, but I just want to see him. I want him to hold me like he did last night. I better go fix myself up so when he returns I look my best.

I'm not alone. Mylow's here today. He has a room downstairs that he uses most of the time he's working from here. I don't have an appetite anymore. I'm so antsy. It's getting late. I've watched everything I could on TV. I'm not sure what's going on or why he's been gone for so long. Maybe I should call him and see if he answers. Then again, maybe he doesn't want anything to do with me right now. He confuses me sometimes with the distance he keeps. I'm not sure how to handle it. I want to be perfect for him, but I'm not. Why am I so emotional? I need to stop crying; it's making my eyes puffy. I wish I were doing a better job. I'll sit and wait. I won't call him. I'll wait until he returns. If he didn't want me here, he could have had Mylow take me home.

The next thing I know, it's night. I must have fallen asleep. I wonder if he's here. He is—I see his shadow moving around in the office. I'll knock on the door, maybe then we can talk.

"I wouldn't do that if I were you!" I spin toward the voice, startled.

"Mylow, you scared me!"

"Ms. Jamie, he's in a bad mood right now. Give him some time. If he is in that study—future advice—don't go in there. If the door is closed, he doesn't want to be disturbed."

"Really? Okay, then I'll wait for him upstairs." I wonder why Mylow would tell me that. I'm learning so much and there's so much more about this man and his life that I don't know. I would have knocked if Mylow hadn't stopped me. Then what? Would Daniel have been even more upset with me? He needs to tell me these things! Maybe Steve was right. Maybe I do talk too much and don't do enough. I'm going to lose him. If that happens, all the things that hateful man said about me would be true. How do I fix this?

"Jamie?"

"Yes?"

"Are you ready to go home?"

"Home...now? But we haven't talked."

"I have a lot going right now. If I don't get you home now, I won't be able to anytime soon. So, the time is now."

"Okay, I guess."

"Mylow said you came down to talk to me. What's going on?"

"I hadn't seen you all day. I wanted to know if you were okay after last night. I was so worried and confused. Daniel, I'm so sorry about last night. Up to that point, I was so happy." I bite my lip, suddenly nervous. "I wanted to tell you… I love you."

He smiles softly and kisses me on the forehead. "I know you do. Come down when you're ready. We have to get going."

Chapter Ten

Summer 1992

Daniel has been so distant. I told him I loved him, but he didn't say it back. When he dropped me off, he said he'd call me and that he knows my mother would be happy to know I was safe. I'm frustrated. My heart is aching for him. I had the time of my life and the worst weekend all at the same time. I'm not sure what this means for us. He left me with a kiss, though. That's all I have to hold to for now. Well, that and his promise to call me.

When I walked in the door, Steve looked at me and smiled like he could sense my insecurities. I could tell he wanted to say something—it was all over his face, but I didn't give him the chance. I headed straight for my room and closed the door. I swear that man could never have kids of his own. He hates too much, too strongly. Maybe I'm wrong. I don't even know anymore. I'm just really frustrated with what happened. I'll patiently wait for Daniel to call me. I'll let him approach me when he's ready. Coming back here and thinking about the best weekend of my life is like a dream turned into a nightmare. I'd be crazy not to want to live with the man I love.

∞∞∞∞

I haven't heard from Daniel in over two weeks. Classes ended for the summer. I'm trying to give him time like Mylow said before I left. Eventually, he will come around. I have to believe that. I miss him, but I'm left wondering where we stand once again. I yearn to be with him, to feel him touch me like he did that night. I need to hear his voice. I'm practically craving it. Just imagining him holding me or thinking about the sound of him on the telephone warms me inside. I don't think I know how to be without him anymore.

I finally give in. It's been almost three weeks and so I called him twice today. He didn't answer the house phone or his car phone. I'm having a hard time functioning. I keep thinking that anytime I go out to do something—grocery shopping, errands for Mama, volunteering—he's going to call. I know he knows I'm calling him. Why does he do this to me? Why is he acting this way? I leave him a message and tell him I need to hear from him and that I miss him. He's going to think I'm clingy and needy. I'm just trying to hold on to him for dear life. He's the best thing that's ever happened to me. I can't believe I'm acting this way.

The days are going by so slow. I now understand why Kelsie had a hard time letting go of Josh in the beginning. Josh made her feel important, so she had given him so much of herself. When they ended, she couldn't find a way to get it back. Should we give anyone that much? I sure wish Daddy were here to help me. I can almost hear him saying, "Take your time, Jamie, and make sure you know what you're doing before you do anything." He would tell me to finish school and focus on my future, to love God with all my heart. But these days are so lonely. I need someone like Daniel who will treat me like a queen and make me feel special, at least some of the time. That's better than nothing.

Mama will one day understand my heart and why I have to do this, that's if she still wants to talk me. Once he calls, I'll tell Mama I'm leaving for good. I can't wait to tell him yes. I have to live my life. I just hope she won't hate me. I'm working hard in school. I want to finish early, but I could use a break this summer. I'll need to get used to my new home, right? This summer will be a much-needed break. I'm not missing school this fall. Most people don't go to school over the summer. I'll still be on track to finish on time.

I'm happy but scared. This could be a life changing moment. I hope I'm doing the right thing. I hope Daniel calls me. He said he'd take care of Mama and anything she needs. I think this is the best choice for both of us. I would do anything for her. I'll finally have the resources to help her. I want to help her, so that maybe she'll see she doesn't need Steve after all.

I know her. She'll think I'm crazy and tell me not to do her any favors. I won't dare tell her. I'll let Daniel surprise her once I'm gone. I'm perfectly capable of making good decisions and choices about my own life. No one tried stopping Kelsie from going to California. Mama certainly didn't approve at first, but Kels went anyway. Look at her now. She's doing fine and is as happy as ever. I wonder if Daniel will always be like this, in and out without a word for weeks at a time. I haven't been sleeping very well—too worried about this mess, I guess.

I lie in bed, worrying and thinking about my own problems when the phone rings. I rush to get it, paranoid it'll stop ringing before I can make it ten feet to the phone. I lift the receiver and hold it to my ear. "Hello?" I ask, excited but terrified.

"Well, hello Ms. Moore. This is Jace, in case you may have forgotten."

I smile despite my bitter disappointment. "I know your voice. How are you?"

"Everything is good—better than I could ask for, really. I'm so glad I caught you."

"Why? What's going on?"

"I was wondering if you're free tonight?"

"Free? Well, yes, I suppose I am."

"I really need some help preparing food boxes for the outreach in the morning. Everyone who signed up to be here, well, isn't. I tried calling everyone." My pride twinges. I don't like being someone's last resort.

"Oh, yes, I can help. Though I'm—"

"I just didn't want to bother you. But, now I'm stuck here and you helped me so much last time. If you can't, of course I understand."

I balance the phone between my ear and my shoulder as I tidy my bedroom and hunt for my sneakers.

"No, Jace, I'll help. I could you use your company tonight too. Can you pick me up?"

"I'll be there in an hour, if that's all right? I promise to have you back by 11."

"Of course, such a gentleman."

"Thank you again, Ms. Moore."

"See you later, Jace!"

No matter how much I'd like to see a friendly face right now, I'm dumbfounded that I agreed to help. What if Daniel calls and I'm not here again? I promised him I'd be here for him if he needed me. But I've waited and waited and he hasn't seen fit to even return one phone call. He has to know the silence and distance is torturing me. But, he does it anyway. I sit on my bed and hang my head in my hands.

I guess this is why Mama hates me being with him. She knows I worry about pleasing him. She wants me to be carefree, but she doesn't know how Steve makes me insane and desperate. I need to get away from him. I'm taking my life seriously. I'm trying to be the woman I should be. The phone rings again. My only thought is that Jace is calling back to cancel because his volunteers decided to show up and he didn't need my help.

"Hello?"

"Hello, pretty lady!"

What awful timing! What am I going to do now? Cancel on Jace just after I agreed to help him?

"Hey, Daniel. How are you? Where have you been?"

"I'm good. Did you decide what you're going to do about moving in with me? I tried to give you enough time to think about it. That way you could be with your mom and figure things out. What did you decide?" *Is that why he's been so distant and refusing to communicate with me? Was he just trying to do what he thought was best for me?* I smile at the thought. He may have been wrong to do it, but he did it with the best intentions, right?

"Yes, I'll move with you, Daniel." I stand up and start pacing.

"Okay, good! You've made your decision—nothing left to say. I'll be there Tuesday evening around four to pick you up." He hesitates for a moment. I almost start to speak. "Jamie, please don't bring any of your old stuff. Leave your clothes and any extra stuff you won't need at your mom's. You have more than enough here a bag or two should be sufficient."

"Daniel, where have you been? I've been calling and calling. I just wanted to hear from you." I looked around my room for a duffle bag to throw my favorite things in, any keepsakes and mementos. Daniel was right— I wouldn't need a lot of my old clothes and shoes. He's already bought me so much new stuff.

"I know you have. We'll have the rest of our lives to be together. I have to go now. I'll see you in a few days."

Well, it's done. He gave me until Tuesday, thank God. I don't know what I would have told Jace if Daniel wanted to pick me up tonight. He really does want what's best for me, I think. Oh no, I have to tell Mama. I should call Kels too. I can't do this without her. No, I can and I will. She didn't need my approval to leave me alone when she left home. But, I need to tell her regardless—it's the right thing to do.

I change into a top more appropriate for moving and filling boxes and my jeans are fine. My nice white sneakers are clean and look good. I stop in front of the mirror to fix my hair and reapply some gloss. Once I'm satisfied, I grab my notebook to jot down some last minute things to remember before Tuesday while I wait for Jace.

He shouldn't be long now. I'm looking forward to spending the evening with Jace. He's such a great listener. I know he'll have some good advice for me. At least I don't have to worry about Daniel calling while I'm out.

I set the book down and roll over with a sigh of relief, too caught up in my thoughts to focus on anything but my new life. I want to be happy and at peace about moving out. I'm sick of beating myself up about everything. I'm lonely here and it's too hard to avoid Steve these days. I can't help but feel like everyone is happy and with someone except me, but not anymore. Now, I don't have just any man, but a good one with money and his own business. I've experienced things people only dream of doing. I wish Mama could see the house for herself. She'd be happy for me then. But she can't and might never be able to freely come by. Daniel said his business just won't allow it, but I still don't know why his business dictates whom I can and can't see. He assures me he will work it out and that I'll be able to see her eventually. I guess that's the part of this that bothers me the most. I don't really understand why Mama can't just come by for a visit. But, living here another week or month with Steve just isn't something I can make myself do—not when I have a better choice. I'm not sure how we could ever peacefully exist in the same space.

It's not long before Jace arrives. I can hear his car pull smoothly into the driveway, but I never hear him knock. After a few minutes, I walk out to the living room.

"Hello, Ms. Moore. How are you?" Jace stands in the entryway talking to my mother.

"I'm good and you?" I step closer to the two of them.

"Quite well. I was just talking to your mom." I raise an eyebrow and turn to my mother, but Jace continues talking. "She was saying she's going to come and visit the church. We talked briefly and she told me some interesting things about you. From what I understand, you're a talented poet, but don't want to admit it." He smiles. "I couldn't agree more with her."

I feel myself flush. "Well, not really. I told you I only write when I'm inspired. I guess I'm okay."

"Jamie, you're better than okay," Jace says seriously. He turns to my mama. "Well, Mrs. Moore, it was a pleasure talking with you, but we must get going. I'll have your very blessed daughter back before too long, if you don't mind?"

"What?" I ask, surprised at his attitude. "Jace, I'm an adult. You don't have to make sure it's okay with my mom!"

"Don't worry about Jamie, honey. It was all in fun. I trust you, so I'll sleep just fine tonight knowing you're looking after her," mama says, smiling. She's never looked at Daniel like that. I wish she would approve of him like she approves of Jace.

I want to bury my face in my hands, but I don't want to mess up my eye makeup either. Instead, I turn to Jace and say, "Shall we?"

We leave the house and head to his car. I climb inside and settle my seatbelt around me.

"Jace, you know that woman loves you." He chuckles politely. "I think she's a great person who loves you and just needs a laugh from time to time. You know she's really quite funny."

"No, actually I didn't know that. It's been a long time since I've seen her sense of humor, but you do have a way of bringing the happy out of folks."

"Enough about me, Jamie. How have you been— really?"

I sigh before saying, "I guess I've been a little restless." I can't keep the happiness off my face when I think about moving out of my mother's house, away from Steve, and being able to see Daniel more often. It'll be nice to be in a home with someone who won't just walk in and ignore me or avoid me for weeks on end as if I'm less than a person.

"Why are you smiling?" the Minister asks. "You have something to tell me?"

I nod. "Yes, but not right now. I want you to talk for a change. You always listen to everyone else and their needs all the time. Tonight I want you to talk to me first."

A small, soft smile crosses his face. "Okay, I will. I want to thank you for coming to help out at the last minute. I didn't know who else to ask. You wouldn't believe how many times God comes through for me."

"You needed me. I'm glad that this time I'm able to help. I've stood you up a few times. I still owe you." We turn into the parking lot and head into the church.

We head into the rec room and Jace gets me to set up empty boxes and fill them with the array of items spread all over the tables that have been donated for the outreach.

After a few moments, Jace says, "Okay, Jamie, I must be honest with you. Only 90% of me needed your help with the meals. But 10% wanted to get you out of the house and see how you were doing. I hope you don't mind." I've never seen the man look so unsure of himself. I'm not really sure why. Jace clears his throat. "Before we get too caught up in what we're doing, what did you want to talk about?"

"I've been contemplating…" I trail off, unsure how to continue. I chance a glance at him as I select items for a box. "No, I'm not contemplating. I've decided I'm moving out of my mother's house. Originally, I wanted to move near campus. I think it's time for me to do my own thing." Jace nodded along understandingly. "I never told you about everything that was going on in my house. Living with Steve is difficult and I can't do it anymore."

"Steve is your mother's boyfriend, right?" he asks.

"Yes. He tortures me with his unkind words and actions. He says the most hurtful things when she's not around. He can go for weeks without speaking to me at all. It seems as if he hates that Kelsie and I are her children. He and Kels did not get along at all. He was so mean to her when she was here. He—" I bite my lip, knowing how this is going to sound. "He'd watch me sleep during the night. I caught him one time. He scares me. It was like he was looking for the perfect time to cut my throat." I turn and look out the window. "Anyway, enough about him. I don't want to talk about him. It's too stressful."

"I'm sorry you've been living like this. You never said anything before. I might have been able to help." Jace touches my shoulder in solidarity. His touch is almost electric and I stifle my reaction.

"I know. I was too ashamed. Mama has some control over him. He'd do whatever Diana Moore tells him to do. She seems to like him around and he helps her a lot. He kind of brought her out of her depression after Daddy died. She met him and she started to come back to the person she used to be. Before Steve, she'd lost all desire to go on. He's helping her, which is why I haven't told her about him. She's happier and starting to live life again." I stop before continuing and turn to him, grinning. "Oh, I see what you're doing, Jace Lawrence. I won't let you off that easy. You did it again. You got me to talk about myself, and my problems, but I said I wanted you to talk. So, go on, start talking, please."

"I will, but it's getting late, Jamie." He looks up, eyes sparkling playfully.

"I don't care as long as we're done before morning, right?"

"Yes, ma'am," he says. We pack another box or two.

"So, what's going with the outreach group?"

Jace tapes a box shut. "It's going okay, but to be honest, Jamie, it's hard to get people to consistently volunteer."

I nod knowingly. My own schedule doesn't allow for very consistent volunteering now that Daniel's back. Even though I want to, the truth is I won't see Jace once I move. Daniel was really clear about my entire life changing and not coming back.

"You know I never get bored with church or with helping others—it's my life. I believe people serve a specific purpose in life. God appoints you to do a certain task designed just for you. And for me, I must obey his will." Jace pauses. "It's like a journey on a bus. You have short stops along the way, but it all falls in line with your purpose—the destination you're trying to reach. There are so many other things I want to do with my life, but this is what I must do for now." He smirks. "I have to complete this assignment before I can move on. Now, let's put these boxes in the hall so they can be loaded into the van for delivery. Then we can get started on the next batch." He shrugs. "My life is extremely boring anyway."

"It's not boring, Jace."

He chuckles. "Okay, if you say so."

We lug the packed boxes into the hall and stack them neatly. Volunteers are supposed to come by in the morning to pick them up and take them to the outreach site for delivery. We don't talk much as we haul the boxes out of the room. When we finish, Jace steps into the small church kitchen and returns with two bottles of water.

"Thanks," I say. He nods as he opens his bottle and takes a large swig.

"I do want to say one more thing to you," he says, wiping water from his mouth. "That gift you gave me has given back to me over and over again."

"It was just a poem," I say, surprised. I fiddle with the bottle cap as I take sips to quench my thirst. I'm glad I changed my shirt. I wouldn't have wanted to get the other one sweaty.

"No, it wasn't. It meant more than that to me. It captured what I wish I could sometimes say to people who look at me and think my life is easy. I meet a lot of young men like me just trying to find direction, but got lost along the way."

"I wrote it with you in mind," I say, unsure of how to respond.

"Yes, I know. I appreciate that."

"You deserve it," I insist.

"I have it hung up in my office. Everyone who reads it asks who wrote it. I'm constantly reminded of you. I wanted to take the time to say that it really blessed me. Thank you, Jamie."

"It's nothing. You just take the simple things people do in life and make them sound extraordinary. Please stop thanking me. I just felt inspired to do it. I don't mind doing things for you because you're someone who appreciates everything, even the small things."

Jace ducks his head a little, pleasantly embarrassed. "Now I'm really smiling. You did that to me. I'm smiling for a lot of reasons though."

I nod and let him have a moment before asking, "How are your parents doing?"

"They're great. My dad just retired as the pastor of his church. He wanted me to fill his position, but I told him no. I think he's disappointed in me, but pastoring isn't my calling. There's too much need on the streets and within the youth community. The young people often get left behind, so I'm doing what I can for them. I call it 'groundwork.'" He reaches for another empty box to pack and assembles it quickly. "I don't know if I shared this with you before, but as much as I love my dad, his life is his own. My life is different and I'm happy with it."

"And your mom? What does she think about it?"

"She supports me in whatever I do. She's my rock. We're close. There's nothing she wouldn't do to protect me." I wish I had that. Kelsie was as close to a rock that I've had since Daddy died. Mama tries, but she has changed so much over the years.

"You have a brother, right?" I ask.

"Yes, he lives in Atlanta. He's done well for himself. He donates to different organizations, including the outreach ministry I do. If it wasn't for his donations, I don't know where the money would come from." Jace gestured around at the donated goods. "People always give stuff—which is great, don't get me wrong—but I need to pay for things too. People often don't really think about where the money comes from."

"That makes sense. Money is harder to come by than donating goods or foods or even your time."

Jace agrees. "I love my brother. He never complains. My sister stays at home raising my niece and nephew. Since she was young, she always wanted to be a mother and wife and God blessed her to be just that. They attend my father's church. My family thinks I'm wasting my time. They believe I should be dating and on the road to marriage with two-point-five kids just around the corner."

"They might be right, Jace. You're a great person and it wouldn't be hard for you to find love. Is that what you want?"

He sets down the box he's filling and turns to face me. "Jamie, I have to live my life the way God would have me to live it," he says, exhaustion leaking into his tone. It doesn't sound like he's tired though, just worn down.

"Okay, I understand. Now that we're on the dating conversation though…" Jace groans not wanting that topic to continue. "I just want to say that you deserve a woman who will love, cherish, and honor you. Someone who will give you all of herself, everything she has to give."

"Jamie, that's very special coming from you."

"There's a 'but' though?"

"Yes, I believe a woman should never give a man—or anyone—her all or everything she has. Where does that leave God? Her family? What about herself?"

I set down the box I'm assembling, intrigued by what he's saying.

"If she's so busy giving me all of what she has, then I'm her God and she is exalting me to a level I can't function on. It's not possible. That's why God should always be first, the only one allowed in that very special heart space." Jace laughs lightly. "I'll happily play second fiddle because I know she's in good hands with God leading. I'm a man. I know I'll will drop the ball from time to time. But that doesn't happen with God. And she needs to make sure she has enough of herself left over for her."

There's so much rushing through my head I can't even process it all. Jace reminds me so much of Daddy. I don't even know where to start. But, what he said also really resonates with me. Is Daniel asking too much of me? I don't know. I don't think so, but maybe he is?

"I'm sorry, Jamie. I didn't mean to go on like that. I want whatever woman I'm dating to feel equally as important in the relationship."

I finally scrape my words together. "Jace, you don't have to say another word. Just the fact that you're that kind of person is so amazing! Most men don't feel that way, I don't think."

"I hope I didn't say anything to offend you. You've got this look on your face right now."

"No, no, not at all. You remind me so much of my daddy and it was like he was speaking through you to me."

Jace looks around at all the goods still to pack. "We should get back to work."

I place my hand on his arm before he can step too far away. "Thank you, Jace, for asking me to come help you tonight. I needed this."

"I've never shared this much of my life with anyone, Jamie. You have a way of getting people to talk to you too. Now, let's get to work."

I laugh and pick up the box I was assembling and start taping it together again. We work hard for a good three or so hours until all the food and household goods have been packed away for the homeless youth. My arms hurt as I struggle to lift the last box onto the pile in the hall. Jace sees what I'm doing and assists. His arms don't shake or waver. Mine feel like spaghetti.

I sag back against the wall. "I can't believe we're done. I thought we'd never finish. All I need now is a pillow and a blanket and a cozy bit of floor right here." Jace laughs.

"I need to lock up and then I'll take you home. Oh, don't think I forgot you had something you wanted to talk to me about too."

Jace closes up the church and I get into the car. He follows me out just a moment later and we buckle in and take off for my house. *Not my house much longer*, I think.

We stop at a red light and Jace says, "What was it you wanted to say?"

I gathered my courage. "As I was saying earlier, my plans were originally to move into my own apartment on campus. But, I've decided to move near Richmond close to Sugarland.

"Richmond? That's the opposite direction from your school," he says, confused.

I shrug. "I know. I never told you, but I've been dating a guy for a while now. He asked me to move in with him."

"What about school?" Jace asks, clearly startled by the news.

"Oh, I'm going back in the fall. I know I'll be living a bit further out, but I'll make the commute work. I'm just taking this summer off." Jace's face has shock written all over it. "Please don't look so surprised."

"What's his name?"

"His name is Daniel." I pause briefly unsure if I should continue my statement. "Jace, he has this gigantic, beautiful, amazing home and he wants to share it with me."

Jace quickly switches his face to neutral.

"He must have one heck of a job," he says after a long moment passes.

"Yes, he owns his own business," I say absently. "Jace, he knows about my living situation and doesn't want me to go on suffering."

"Well, I can't argue with that—"

"But you want to?" Jace doesn't say anything. "I've never been in a home like his before and now I have a

143

chance to live in one. I want to experience every opportunity life gives me."

"Are you sure?" he asks, his voice quiet, strong, and solemn.

I avert my gaze from his. "No, I mean, yes, I've thought about it and living with Steve any longer—even another week—would drive me crazy." I take a deep breath, steadying myself. I'm not sure why I'm so nervous and anxious about this. "I haven't told Mama my plans yet, which is my problem. There's so much more out there than what I've seen and I want to see it all—to live the best life I can." I take a chance and look back at him. He's focused on the road. "This is the most I've shared with anyone other than Daniel. You make it easy, Jace, too easy."

"So, when are you leaving?" He turns down the main road that leads to my house.

"Tuesday. I leave Tuesday."

Jace turns away from the road and looks me square in the eye for several moments longer than is comfortable, considering he's driving. "You're serious?" I nod. He turns back to the road. "This must have been planned for a while." His eyes flick to me. I shrug. "Jamie, do you love him?"

I fidget in my seat. "Yes, I believe so. I've never been in a relationship before, so I don't have anything to compare it to, I guess. But, I do know I want to be with him. He isn't as transparent as I would like. He's a very private person. He told me my life as I know it will change. I won't be able to come around like this anymore. I have to be away from Mama for a while; it's a sacrifice I have to make. There's a lot about his life I don't know, especially about his business and all. But, he's good to me and he has taken me places I've never been before." Jace nods stiffly. I swallow hard. "I'm sorry. Here I am going on and on..."

Jace pulls into my driveway and turns the car off. He turns to me fully. "Jamie, I want nothing more than to see you happy. If he makes you happy, then I'm overjoyed for you. But," Jace hesitates, and switches to his 'minister' voice, strangely calm, "why live together? Why not just move into an apartment near your school?" I scramble, trying to understand Jace's attitude. He's being nothing but supportive, if curious, but I can't shake the feeling he thinks I've made the wrong decision. I just don't know why.

"He wants me with him all the time. He doesn't want me riding the bus or catching rides. He lives a certain way, Jace." I sigh. "And, I guess, he wants us to live that way together."

Jace purses his lips in thought before saying, "Jamie, have you thought about what God would want you to do in this situation? Anything worth having is worth waiting for."

I'm taken back. What's he saying? "What are you trying to say?" I ask, confused more than defensive.

"Nothing, I'm sorry. I shouldn't have said anything."

"Come on, explain what you meant, please."

Jace takes a deep breath. "If you want it badly enough, you'll wait to make sure it's really as good as you think it is."

I fiddle with my purse strap. "So, you think I should wait and test the waters? He's an impatient man. He can have any woman in the world he wants. I have no grounds to keep him waiting on me to figure my life out."

Jace opens his mouth to say something, but I start again before he can get the words out. "I appreciate talking with you tonight. It's been full of positive emotions and so much fun—relaxing even. It's refreshing being with you. You've given me so much to think about tonight. I have to really spend some time working through everything putting things into perspective before I leave in a few days."

"Of course, Jamie. You're welcome." He hesitates again. Why does he keep watching his words that way? "I think you know your mom would be worried about you. I also think there will be no easy way to break this to her."

I wrap my arms around myself tightly and stifle tears. "Jace, please pray for me. I'm scared that I'm not going to be enough for him. I'm afraid my mother might regress when I leave. I can't bear to see her depressed like that again. I know Steve is with her and she likes him. I know I can't live another week with that man in my house.

"Of course I'll pray for you, Jamie. You're always in my prayers."

I smile at him, sincerely touched. "I have one more thing to ask of you, Jace." He nods as I bite my lip, embarrassed. "Would you check on my mother from time to time? Please make sure she's okay. I won't be able to come by once I leave."

With this confession, alarm springs onto his face and I hold up a hand.

"It's a long story. I can't explain it right now. He has a complicated life and his business requires a lot of privacy for many reasons beyond my control. Will you promise me you'll come by here and check on her?"

"Yeah, I will. I promise to come by and see her."

I sigh with relief; a tightness in my chest easing that I didn't even know was there. "Thank you so much. I couldn't ask for a better friend than you. Daniel's going to make sure all of her financial needs are taken care of each month. So, it's worth it to me."

"Jamie, will you do me a favor?"

"Of course, Jace. What is it?"

"Pray. Pray hard and make sure it's Gods voice you're listening to before you move on Tuesday. Could we even pray together before you go inside?"

"Yes, I'd like that very much."

147

"Father God, I come to you—we come to you asking you for nothing but direction, understanding, and clarity. Ms. Moore is making life-changing decisions. So please, God, guide her path and clear her mind so she may make righteous decisions. Please, God, protect her body, mind, and soul. Heavenly Father, we don't take you for granted. Give us a praying spirit so we can seek you for ourselves. Give her the peace that surpasses all understanding. Help her come to grips with whatever decision is made in her household. Give her the strength and the tenacity to fight through whatever battles come her way. Lord, I pray that in her quiet place, the voice that meets her in her sleep is yours. In Jesus's name, amen. "

"Amen," I reply in kind, quietly.

"Jamie, I'll be praying for you. I want you to be okay. I want you to be safe. Even though I won't see you, I'll always be praying for you."

I carefully wipe my eyes and hold back tears. "Thank you."

"Let your tears flow. You can cry. It's okay. In life, we all are going to make some decisions we aren't entirely comfortable with, but we figure it out."

"Jace, you are so good inside. I want you to know that every time I've been around you, I've felt such a sense of peace. One day, when it's time, you'll find love and happiness. Thank you again for being my friend and for all of the times you've prayed for me and my family."

Loneliness Within

"It was my pleasure. You're a great person, Ms. Moore, one of a kind. That Daniel sure is blessed to have you in his life and—" Jace stopped, swallowing his words. "And—"

"What is it? Go ahead, Jace."

"Nothing. It's nothing."

"I know that I've asked a lot of you."

"Don't worry about that, Jamie! I've already promised I'll come by and check on your mom. She's on my personal prayer list now."

I tug the door handle, opening the door. "It's late. I better get inside and get some rest." I lean across the console between the seats and quickly kiss him on the lips this time. "Goodbye, Jace." He sits there, unmoving, as I walk up to the house. Once I'm inside, I chance a quick look outside and see him shake his head in what I think was disbelief before starting the car.

Oh God, I'm so confused right now. He's a Minister—one of your own. I'm such a bad person. I don't know why I did that, but I wanted to kiss him. Oh God, please forgive me. I'm so sorry. He deserves so much more than that. God, please give him what his heart truly desires. He's a good and honest person and deserves so much more.

I look at the clock on the mantle before deciding that I'll have to tell Mama in the morning. I say another prayer for her to understand that I have to do this.

149

Chapter Eleven

Mama isn't talking to me, not since our conversation earlier. This morning, I gathered my courage and finally told her I'm moving in with Daniel. Steve couldn't wait to jump in and give his unwanted comments. But more than what he said, the look on his face said everything I needed to know. He was so excited that it was insulting. I called Kelsie and got her voicemail, so I left her a message telling her that I was leaving. I explained that Daniel will take good care of me and not to worry. I said I'll have everything in the world I could want or need. I also told her that I won't be back to this house for a long time. I need a break and Mama needs time to heal. Maybe the distance will help her understand. I wish I could have talked to her, but sometimes it's days before I can get a hold of her. She's been really busy out there in California. On the message, I told Kels that she needed to check on Mama more often and call every chance she gets. I hope she does.

I keep thinking I'm being selfish, but why? I refuse to live here with him anymore. I have Daniel now and a magnificently beautiful home to live in. This is my life now. I can't even describe my joy—it just bubbles up and overflows within me. I told Mama I'll send her money to cover whatever she needs and that she doesn't need to worry about bills anymore, despite my original plan not to say anything. She looked at me and said she was so disappointed. She insisted that she'll make it without me and she doesn't want *his* help. Just as I thought, she wants nothing to do with Daniel or his money. I'm trying to help her, but she doesn't see it that way.

This is good for me. Isn't it? I'm not so sure because I've been crying for the last three hours. I look around this old place and feel so many emotions. I'll miss my home. I grew up here. I played in this house with my family as a child. My daddy raised us here. The back porch has a gorgeous view of the sparkling night stars. The old house has so many nooks and crannies that only Kelsie and I know about. I have so many memories here. I'll cherish every one of them forever. Why is this so hard? Shouldn't I be happy about it?

I pack all of my stuff into boxes and put them in the back of the closet. I won't need any of this old stuff. I'm only taking my pictures and the Bible Daddy bought me when I started kindergarten. I want to leave everything else just the way it is. I guess Mama can use this as a guest room or something. I don't know. These are going to be the longest three days of my life.

∞∞∞

I wake up Tuesday morning with a smile on my face. I can't believe today is the day I'm moving out. Mama won't talk to me. She won't even look at me. Her silence is forcing me even farther away. Mama needs to live for herself and find her own way in life. I'll never be okay with not seeing her, but Daniel promised he would work things out. I want to believe Steve will disappear, but that's not likely. Kelsie's mad at me too. After I told her what I was doing, she was furious and said she was coming to visit as soon as she could.

This isn't fair to me. How does finding love mean I'm a bad daughter and that I don't love Mama? I pray between Steve, Ms. Marie, Jace, and Kelsie that Mama will be fine. She'll have more support than I will. I'll only have Daniel.

I sigh and take a quick look around my bedroom, making sure I haven't left anything crucial behind. Nope, nothing. I should really try talking to Mama again before I go. I walk down the hallway and knock softly at her door.

"Mama, I need to talk to you before he gets here." Nothing. I sigh and continue. "Are you sleeping? I know you can hear me." Still no response, well, it's no wonder where Kelsie gets her stubbornness. "Mama, I want you to know that I'm not leaving you. I just think its best that I move out. I know I said it would be near campus, but Daniel asked me to move into this amazing house with him and he's been so good to me." I shuffle my feet. "You don't like him. I get that, Mama, but you never gave him a chance. You think he is hiding things, but I believe in him and I trust him. He's not perfect, but who is? I have an opportunity to be with the man I love. I thought you'd understand at least that much. I promise I'll make you proud of me."

I can hear a quiet shuffle behind the closed door. Then, after a moment's hesitation, the door opens and Mama stands there, stone-faced.

"I'll have Daniel come by and bring you over to the house soon, okay?" Mama's face grimaces. "Trust me like you trusted Kelsie when she went all the way to California. Look at how well she's done. I love you, Mama. I'll write you all the time. I'm sorry I won't be able to visit. He is very busy and we will be traveling, but I'll do what I can."

Mama frowns. "Be happy and take care of yourself. I'll always be with you in heart." I try to catch her eye, but she won't even look at me. I sigh.

"You're a stubborn woman, you know that? I know Steve will do anything for you, but I've been in the way, Mama. I can't really explain everything that I'm feeling right now, but all I want is for you to understand that I have to do this." I pull her into a hug and she squeezes me back tightly. It's the only indication that she still loves me. Mama jumps when someone knocks on the door.

"I think that's Daniel."

I hug her once again, quickly, and dart to the living room door.

"Hey, Daniel. I'm sorry it took so long. I was in the back talking to Mama. She's not really accepting that I'm leaving.

"Jamie, you can always stay with your mom if you think that would be best for her."

I cast a quick look over my shoulder. "No," I whisper. "I have to make a life of my own. I want to do this. I refuse to live here another day if I don't have to. It's going to take her a while to get over it, but everyone's agreed to make sure she's okay." I take a deep breath. "Would you mind going in and saying something to her?" Daniel grumbles.

"Jamie, me telling your mother that I won't hurt you isn't going to change anything. She feels the way she does because she wants you to be right here with her forever. Nothing I can say will change that. She doesn't like me," he sighs, "but, if it pleases you, I'll go in and talk to her."

I smile and kiss him on the cheek. "Thank you, Daniel. I'd appreciate that." He nods and walks to the kitchen where Mama has been casually eavesdropping.

"Hello, Mrs. Moore. I apologize if I'm intruding on your cooking." Mama barely acknowledges him. "Jamie's a great person. I care deeply for her and she'll be in good hands with me. I'll take care of her." He smiles, as charming as ever. "Ma'am, please know there's nothing I wouldn't do to protect her. I understand that I might not be your choice as a son-in-law, but this is her decision. This will always be her home. I wish you and Steve well and I hope you have a happy life together. Is there anything you want to say to me?"

Mama says nothing, just stares at him as she slices up vegetables for a salad.

Daniel coughs awkwardly. "Well, we're going to leave now."

Steve comes into the kitchen from the outside and grins at Daniel. I can't manage to hold my tongue anymore.

"You have her all to yourself now, Steve. You better take care of my mother or you'll answer to me. Have a good life, you sick old man!" I turn to Daniel and bury my face in his shoulder. "Let's go, please."

He nods and leads me outside. He gets me settled into the car and then brings the few things I wanted to take with me out to the car too.

Daniel gets into the car as I wipe my face clean of tears, careful not to smudge my makeup.

"I hate that man. Did you see that look he had on his face? He was so delighted. Please make sure he's good to her and that she's taken care of like you promised. Please?"

"Jamie, I said that I'd take care of her and I will. You need to focus on your new life. Erase all of those thoughts and memories of when you lived with that man and all the struggling you've had to do. Now, you can look forward to your future and what I need you to be for me. You're important and now a part of my inner circle. Can you focus on me now?"

"Yes, definitely. I'm sorry. I know you're tired of hearing me go on and on about my life. I won't bring it up anymore, I promise. All I want to do is make you happy. I just have so many emotions going through me right now."

"Jamie, I've been patient, but now it's time for you to put that behind you." I nod and spend the rest of the drive trying to calm down and let it all go. I don't want to walk through the door to my new home with tears running down my face. I need to be stronger.

After the long drive, we pull into the driveway and I quietly get out of the car. Hand-in-hand, we go inside.

"It's so much different now. Walking through the door and knowing this is my home. Before, I was shocked that you were a part of this world, one I'd never seen before. And then finding out you made a home for me was beyond my understanding. I'm so lucky to have you. This is where we live now, together."

"Yes, this is real for both of us. I want to talk to you later, but I'll let you get settled first. Before we go to dinner, there are some home security things you need to know. Go on upstairs. Freshen up and meet me downstairs in an hour."

"Sure, I'll see you then." I walk calmly up the stairs and head to our bedroom.

He's a very direct person, but he said that the first day I met him. Who am I to complain? I love him. No one else that I know has ever had the man they love do the things for them that he's done for me. He's so giving and not just to me, but he's willing to do the same for my mother. He's complicated, though, very busy and private too. But, I'm learning I have to understand that this is the grown up world and we don't always get everything how we want it.

I can't wait to spend time with him alone again. That man made me feel things I never knew my body was capable of. I can't stop thinking about it. I'll do what he said and put all my memories behind me.

I'm looking forward to dinner tonight. While we were in the car, Daniel mentioned that Mylow is joining us for dinner. And I'll get to find out what Daniel was talking about when he said he had something he wanted to discuss with me. I'm not worried, though. I think it'll be good news. It'll be nice to see Mylow again. He has such an interesting job. I don't know how he does it. Looking after Daniel must be so hard. He's always so busy with work. Then again, they've been this way for years. They originally met at a military base in California where they were stationed. Daniel said they've been through a lot together. Mylow's like the brother he never had.

I set my few things down around the room and thoroughly explore my new clothes and freshen up. Unsure of what else I should do, I decide to pick up a book from the small bookshelf in the sitting nook and read through it. After it's been about an hour, I head downstairs. Daniel is in the dining room.

"Jamie, come sit with us. I was just talking with Mylow before you came down. I want to talk with you about the rules and what I expect from you within this house." I nod and sit down next to him. "From this point on, you cannot communicate with anyone you know outside of us."

My mouth just fell open in shock. "What?" I ask, dumbfounded. "I have to check on my mom from time to time, at the very least."

"Yes, I understand that and we will work that out when the time comes, but no one else. It's too complicated."

What does he mean? Why can't I talk to anyone?

Daniel ignores my shocked expression and continues on, "You're not cleared to go outside of this house unless Mylow is with you. A part of my job is to keep you safe. You're very important in my life. Don't make this hard on me, okay?"

"Yes, Daniel." What else can I say to that? I don't have a car. This house is too far from a bus stop. Where would I even go without Mylow?

"I don't want you working around the house. Ms. Janice does the cleaning. She comes to the house three times a week to clean. Other than Ms. Janice, no one else is allowed to enter this home under any circumstances. I travel very often—sometimes for weeks at a time. Please forgive me in advance. If I didn't think you could handle it, I wouldn't be with you. Do you understand?"

Understand what? That he'll be gone a lot? I knew that. I guess I just thought I'd be talking to other people too. "Yes, Daniel."

"Good. Mylow will be with you most of the time. He is your go-to person in case I can't be reached, and most of the time, that will be the case. Please know this is a commitment and I told you before it's not going to be easy. Anything you want is yours. Just let Mylow know if you want to go shopping or go out for lunch or dinner. He'll drive you. When I'm home, I prefer to order dinner in. You can feel free to do the same. Whatever you want, Mylow can have it delivered. I don't have a chef—it's too much of a hassle."

I nod, just trying to keep up. I can't imagine just ordering delivery all the time. We hardly ever ate out growing up. It was a treat, not something we just did. Mama cooked most of the meals I've eaten in my life. Daniel hesitates, noticing he's lost my undivided attention. I smile at him sheepishly.

"Jamie, you're a key piece of my life. I really want you to know that."

"Daniel, I do know that. I know you care about me, that I'm important to you. I wouldn't have moved in with you if I didn't think so."

"Do you have any questions?" he asks, touching my hand.

"No, I understand."

He nods, satisfied. Mylow clears his throat and raises his eyebrows.

"Oh, one more thing—my office is completely off limits to anyone. If I'm in there, just wait for me to come out. I conduct a lot of important business in there and I can't be disturbed for anything other than an absolute emergency when I'm in there with the door closed."

"I'll remember that."

"Oh, I almost forgot. There are no phone lines in this house. Well, there's one in my office, but it is off limits except for absolute emergencies—like a fire. Mylow has a cellular phone for business and to keep in contact with me."

I'm stunned. No phone line? But how am I supposed to get in touch with my family at all? I know he said no communication, but he also said we'd figure out a way to make it work. Daniel catches my chin in his hand.

"Hey, don't look so sad. I told you before that life with me comes with sacrifices."

I nod and turn my head away, trying to ignore the tears threatening to fall. A feeling of loneliness instantly overtook me.

"Smile—we're going to dinner tonight, just you and me. I have a surprise for you." I lift my head toward him and offer him the best smile I can. I feel like instead of starting a new life, my life has fallen apart.

∞∞∞

Last night was so wonderful. It was romantic and sweet. I'm so comfortable with him. I can't imagine being with anyone else in that way. He makes me feel so wanted and needed. I love him so much. He gave me a gorgeous diamond bracelet. I've never worn anything like it. I could never repay him for everything he's offered me. He slept in bed with me last night, peacefully too. I finally got the chance to sleep with him all night. I've never been so relaxed. He cuddled me close and I fell asleep with his sweet nothings in my ear. I guess his nightmares are getting better. Just knowing I woke up in the arms of the man I love is like a dream.

∞∞∞

After living with Daniel for a few months, I've decided I need a hobby to occupy my time. I like to shop, but it's not something I can do every day. And when Daniel is away, I'm bored out of my mind. I know I can read and exercise, but I want something different. I've been thinking about practicing cooking. I'm a decent cook, at least that's what Mama always said, but I'd like to be better. I want to surprise Daniel with home cooked food when he comes home. I think next time Mylow and I go out we'll stop by the bookstore and get a few cookbooks.

Ms. Janice couldn't be more kind. She's as sweet as honey, as my grandma used to say. Yesterday, she brought me a rice cake she made from scratch. She has an accent, but her English is so good I hardly notice it sometimes.

Daniel had to leave for a work trip a couple of weeks ago. I've spoken to him on the phone only once in the last few weeks. Oh my, I miss him more than I can say. The bed is so big and empty without him. I'm glad I didn't have much of a chance to get used to having him next to me at night. Thankfully, he assured me he'll be home soon. I know he told me he travels all the time for work, but I don't understand why I have to be alone most of the time. I miss him and I miss Mama too. I want to call her, but Mylow said I can't right now. He thinks I should give her time to process everything and that I should send her a postcard or a letter and something special in the mail. I think he might be right. I didn't want to cause any trouble or make our relationship worse, so today, I wrote to her.

Dear Mama,

I pray you are well. I miss you and I hope you aren't terribly mad at me. I want you to know I had to move like I did for so many reasons. I needed to break away and be free to grow and learn who I am as a person. I was lost after Daddy died. I spent so much time covering up my pain. The honest truth is if I didn't leave when I did, things would have gotten worse and I didn't want to do that to you. I know you don't trust or like Daniel, especially now that you might blame him from taking me away from you. But it wasn't his decision—it was mine and mine alone. If I had a chance to do it over again, I would make the same choices. I am happy with him. Mama, we live in a home as beautiful as the one Grandma cleaned. Daniel said he'd arrange for us to talk, but I know how stubborn you are and that you don't want him around. But unless you can find a way to like him, Mama, we'll continue to be distant. He is the man I love and this is my life now. Please try to be happy for me. I understand if you can't now, but maybe one day.

I love you and Kelsie. No one will ever change that!

Love,

Jamie

I tuck the letter into an envelope and put it right on top of everything so it'll be the first thing she sees. I send her some rolls of fabric, thread, and needles for her machine. I know she'll love it. I wonder what she'll make with the fabric.

I overheard Mylow talking to Daniel about arranging transportation from the airport. He sent a car to pick Daniel up over an hour ago, so he should be home soon. I'm so excited that my man will be home tonight. I'm also really happy I had the hairdresser at the mall fix my hair this afternoon. It was spur of the moment, but I want to look really good for him. I need him to remember me when I'm looking good so he won't forget that I'm all the woman he needs.

I'm in the bedroom when I hear the front door open, but by the time I make it downstairs, he and Mylow have shut themselves in his office. I'm standing in the hall, unsure of what to do. I can hear him talking to Mylow, but I can't make out what they are saying through the door, other than something to do with the business. I'm much too busy minded to sit around here and wait. I'm not sure what else to do though. I want to see him. He's hardly ever around and I don't like being kept quiet and alone in this house. Oh, how I long to see him, to feel his embrace. From the sound of it, they're going to be in the office for a while and I look crazy standing out here, just waiting around to see him. Maybe I'll head up to the study to read for a while.

I walk in and select a book off the shelves, just something to flip through to pass the time, but soon I'm engrossed and several chapters in. I look to the grandfather clock and notice it's been over an hour. What on earth are they talking about in there?

I replace the book on the shelf and wander back toward the office just as the door opens. Daniel's in the middle of saying something, but I don't know what they're talking about—just that he sounds mighty frustrated.

"Hey, pretty lady. You miss me?" he asks, reaching for me and pulling me close.

"Yes! I missed you so much. I'm so happy to have you home," I mumble into his shoulder, burying my face in his scent.

"Go on upstairs and wait for me. I'll be up in a minute." I nod as he pulls away from me. A sly grin crosses his face. "Jamie, you look great!"

"Thank you," I say flirtatiously. As I head upstairs, I can't stop thinking that I shouldn't be so needy for his attention. He'll get bored with me if I act like that. I want him to know I love him, but also that I'm able to take care of myself. I want him to know I'm strong. I wonder how long it's going to be before he has to leave again.

∞∞∞∞

I shouldn't have been surprised. Weeks have passed, and other than the occasional night spent between here and the condo in the city, Daniel's never home. I'm

165

starting to believe he likes the distance between us. I think I saw him more often when we didn't live together. This isn't what I expected, but I guess none of it has been. I know I'm still learning, still adjusting to the new situation. I should be patient. This living situation is new to both of us. Maybe his business calls for him to spend a lot of nights in the city; the condo seems to be more convenient for him. I keep telling myself not to worry about it—Mylow doesn't seem concerned.

Ms. Janice will be here tomorrow, so I can talk to her. Last time we were talking, I told her she was a historian in another life and she laughed so loud. She knows Daniel and Mylow pretty well because she's been working here for over two years. I know Daniel appreciates her loyalty. I'm so impressed by Ms. Janice. She's such a strong beautiful spirited lady. She has two children and a dog and she's had to work very hard to support her family because she divorced her husband after he up and left her and their children to move back to Venezuela.

She said the one decent thing he did before he left was give her all the money he'd saved up, but when it was gone, she had to find work to support herself and her children. I told her I'd hate the man who did that to me, but she doesn't. She said living in the States wasn't working for him. Then, he started drinking and she realized he had to go sooner than later. She says it was the best thing for her and the kids. It's so sad. She works hard around here and then goes home and has to parent her young kids all on her own. I admire her and I want to help her any way I can. I try to help her out by cleaning up after myself more.

I hear the front door open and a smile breaks across my face. Daniel comes up the stairs just as I exit the bedroom. He kisses the top of my head and goes to the end room, leaving the door cracked.

"How's it going, pretty lady?" he calls through the door. I stand in the bedroom, waiting.

"I've been getting by," I say.

"Just getting by?" he asks.

"It's hard being here without you, without anyone really. I think it would help if I could talk to Mama, at least to say hi."

"Jamie, listen to me," he says, coming back into the bedroom. "I know this is hard, but you have to be strong. When I get back from this trip, we'll arrange something."

"I just miss you so much when you're gone."

"I know you do." He pulls me into a passionate kiss, but before I can get too caught up, he steps back. "Mylow's downstairs ordering dinner. You should tell him if there's something special that you want. I'll be back before the food gets here.

"Wait, where you going?"

"Out. Jamie, I'll be right back."

As he leaves, I'm pretty sure he isn't coming back tonight. I check myself in the mirror and then head downstairs to talk with Mylow. He placed the order for dinner, and when it arrived an hour later, we ate without Daniel. I put Daniel's meal in the fridge so it wouldn't go bad. I didn't have much of an appetite. I still don't.

Maybe I'm too needy? Am I bothering him when he comes home? Is that why he's been spending more and more time away? I'm not sure if he's out of town or at the condo. I'm so sick of being alone. I'm finding it harder and harder to eat, to get out of bed. Normal life just isn't interesting anymore. I really want to be with him more, but now he's gone once again. There's only so long I can wait up for him.

I guess I fell asleep on the sofa, waiting for him to come home. I hear the shower running upstairs, so I get to my feet and head up there. The light is on in the room at the end of the hallway, it's Daniel. I change into my pajamas and crawl into bed. He must have just gotten in, but it's nearly three o'clock in the morning. What was he doing out so late? Who was he with? If he was in the city, why didn't he just stay at the condo? I look around the room and see that he left his clothes in a pile on one of the sitting nook chairs. Peering through the darkness, I wonder where he got the tux. That wasn't what he was wearing when he left.

Plus, I thought he said he was running out and coming back right back? He's been out somewhere nice enough for him to need a tux. Why didn't he say that? Why

168

didn't I go with him? I guess he didn't want me to, but why not? With how secretive he is, I may never know. I wouldn't dare ask; it would upset him.

Daniel exits the bathroom having already turned the light off and doesn't notice me on the sofa. He shuts the bedroom door behind him, but I can already hear the guest-room door shut down the hall. I guess he's not sleeping in here tonight. I can't think about this right now, but this is hurtful. I wipe my tears away in the dark.

Meant for Love

Love is a bit over rated it seems,
But still,
We joy in the illusion and obscure signs.
Love is defined in the good book as enduring and caring.
Can someone tell me why cupid isn't sharing?
The mystery,
This notion of a sentimental connection with another,
Can this be something more than a simple bed lover?
Sure it is,
We were created to find,
That one that makes our clock unwind.
The flesh,
The heart that was designed to display its gentle kind
nature,
Love is uncertain at first,
Complicated at best,
But, we must have it,
It's by design.
God knew its worth to us,
It was meant for us,
It is much more.

Chapter Twelve

December 1992

    I thought I could handle life with Daniel, but it's been almost seven months since I moved in. I've only seen him a few times a month. When he's home, he typically spends his nights with me, but he still leaves for weeks at a time. He says he really cares about me, that I'm so important to him, but I can't tell anymore. Am I the only woman for him? When he makes love to me, it feels like love. He's so passionate and intense. He makes me feel like I'm the only one for him, but then it's over.

    After spending an evening or two together, I might not see him for weeks at a time. How can I be so important to a man I'm not around most of the time? Is there more to his life than what he shares with me? There must be if it keeps him so far away from me.

    I can't help but wonder if Mama was right—maybe he does have family somewhere else. I've never seen the condo in downtown Houston. Mylow tells me we aren't allowed to go there. I'm definitely not getting used to this, not at all. I haven't been in school either, which is driving me crazy. I write to stay sane. I can't believe I missed the fall semester. I'm falling behind now and I won't be able to graduate early.

I love the days Ms. Janice comes. She'll be here soon, actually. At least I can talk to her when she's done cleaning. The other day she told me I was smart and that I should be looking into going back to school as soon as possible. I told her that I wished it was that easy. Spring semester is approaching and I need to get back to it.

Last night, I asked Mylow to call Daniel for me. He did, but he said Daniel didn't answer or call back. He talks with him sometimes, just not about me going back to school. I can't get too upset with Mylow, though. It's not his fault. He does whatever Daniel tells him to do. When Daniel returns, I'll tell him how I'm feeling myself. I feel like he hasn't upheld his end of the deal. Every time I try to talk him about things like school or talking to Mama, he brushes me off and gets agitated.

Mama probably hates me by now. I send her gifts, but she can't respond because she doesn't have my address. I didn't want her coming by and making it hard on me, so I never gave it to her. Plus, Mylow asked me not to put the address on anything I send to her for security reasons. All of the secrets, the hiding, the monitored lifestyle, I'm really irritated with it all. I wonder if Daniel has sent her any money. I haven't heard anything about it since the day I left. I can't believe I chose this crazy life. I wish I knew how to fix it.

∞∞∞

Today, Mylow told me, much to my surprise, that Daniel is coming home for a few days. Then, Mylow said he was going to leave and that he'd be back in a few hours, but he hasn't left yet. I suppose he had to get ready first and just wanted to let me know in case I needed something. He told me not to go outside at all, not even on the patio. I wish I knew why they seem to think it's so unsafe without someone home to protect me. I've never seen anything alarming happen on this street. I haven't seen anyone trying to break in or vandalize the house. There's no one invading our privacy. We have an alarm that would alert us to anything like that too. I hope things get better soon. I don't think I can take much more of it.

Strange things are going on, but it doesn't bother me much. Mostly, my issues are with Daniel. The last time he was home, he was in a rage about something that happened. I overheard him telling Mylow that business was getting bad and that something needed to change. I hope it changes real soon. I want my life to be different.

I walk downstairs and stand in front of Daniel's closed office door. All right, that's it. I'm calling Mama today once Mylow leaves. I've been so patient waiting for Daniel to work it all work out, but I'm done waiting. Damn the rules at this point! As soon as he leaves, I'm going into Daniel's office and calling her. I'll come right out and I won't touch anything but the phone. It won't take me very long, but I'll finally get to hear her voice! It's been too long. I miss her so much. I need to know she's okay and I want her to know I'm okay. She hasn't heard my voice since the day I left. For all she knows, I could be dead.

"Jamie?" Mylow calls.

"Yes?"

"I'm heading out now. I'll be back in a couple of hours."

"All right."

"Stay inside, please."

"I will," I say with a smile. Mylow nods and exits through to the garage. A few moments later, I hear the car start and can see him turn out of the driveway and head down the street. I make sure to wait a ten minutes to be sure he hasn't forgotten anything. When he doesn't come back, I head to the office door.

Come on, Jamie, I coach myself. Why are my hands shaking? I'm going in to make this call and no one can stop me. I'm not hurting anyone by doing this.

I turn the knob and gently push into the office. I see his phone on the desk where it always is and walk over to it. I lift the receiver and quickly punch in Mama's number. It rings for a minute before I hang up. I contemplating going back upstairs, but I think I'll try Ms. Marie's number first. Thankfully, the phone rings for just a second before she answered.

"Hello?"

"Hello, Ms. Marie."

"Hi, who is this?"

"Oh, sorry. This is Jamie Moore from down the street."

"Oh hey baby, how are you? I haven't seen you in quite some time."

"I'm good, Ms. Marie. And you?"

"I'm doing just fine. Same old, same old, you know?"

I chuckle. "I'm calling because I dialed my mama's number and no one is answering. I was wondering if you've talked to her lately?"

"Oh, you haven't talked to Diana then I see." She sounds slightly uncomfortable, but I'm not sure why. I hope Mama's okay.

"No, ma'am, I haven't. What's wrong?"

"Oh, nothing's wrong, Jamie. Your mom is just staying at a hotel not 'too far away temporarily. She's been there for over a month now."

"What happened? Is it the house? Is she okay?"

"Don't worry, child. Your mama is doing just fine. Her old house is under renovation."

"Renovation? Did something happen?" I ask, unable to keep the worry and confusion out of my tone.

"Well, not exactly. An unknown sponsor gave your mother a check to have her house completely remodeled. Can you believe that? She is a blessed woman. Not only did they pay for the renovations, but they paid off her mortgage entirely too. Folks from her job donated to help pay for the hotel until its ready." I can't believe it. I'm stunned. I can't make myself say anything. "Can you hear me? Jamie, you there?" Ms. Marie asks.

I wipe my tears away and take a deep breath before I can speak. "Yes, ma'am, I'm here. I'm just speechless."

"God sent that woman an angel. Lord knows she deserves it," Ms. Marie says decidedly.

"I'm sorry, but I have to go now, Ms. Marie. I'll call you back as soon as I can to get the number to the hotel where I can reach her. Thank you so much for telling me. You've made my day—no, my week. I'm so pleased Mama is happy and doing well. Thank God, Ms. Marie."

"Okay, baby. I'll have the number for the hotel when you call me back."

"Oh, Ms. Marie, please don't tell Mama I called. I want to surprise her. I want her to enjoy herself without worrying about me."

"Of course, Jamie, if that's what you want," she says, a slight stiffness to her voice.

"Thank you again!"

"Okay, bye baby!"

I have to keep calm. I need to act like everything is the same, but I can't believe this! Daniel is the most amazing man ever. He's the only person who could afford to pay for something like that. How could I have ever doubted him? He must really love me. Whether he says it or not, I know he does now. God, I promise I'll work really hard not to upset him and I'll show him how grateful I am from now on. I wish I could thank him, but he can't know I found this out. He'd immediately know I went against his wishes by going into his office and calling her. I definitely crossed the line there and I must keep it to myself. But, I'm so happy right now!

When Mylow gets home, I catch him before he can disappear into his room.

"Hey, Mylow, I have a question."

"Sure, what's up?" he says as he takes off his heavy winter coat.

"Do you think Daniel will be home for Christmas this week? He wasn't for Thanksgiving, but I'd like it if we could have Christmas together."

"Yeah, I think so. He usually makes a point to take some time off this time of year. It's a little tough for him since his parents aren't around. They always did something special together over the holidays, so it's more than likely he'll be around."

I can't help my grin. "Okay, good. I want to do something special for him. I want to surprise him for once."

"That's going to be hard, Ms. Jamie. He likes to know everything."

I nod. "I know. That's why I need your help."

"Of course, I'll help any way I can. I'm sure he'll appreciate whatever you do."

"Then could we start tonight? I'd like to make dinner for him before he gets home. Will you help me?

"Sure, Ms. Jamie," Mylow says as he follows me into the kitchen.

Together, Mylow and I whip up a fantastic meal. We have grilled steak, steamed vegetables, red potatoes, an apple pie Mylow bought from his favorite bakery, cranberry juice instead of wine, accompanied by warmed, honey-buttered dinner rolls. Mylow arranged for a car to pick him up, so he doesn't have to go and get him, which gives us some extra time to put together the meal. When Daniel gets home, he talks with Mylow for a few minutes about business, but then I call to him from the dining room, hoping they weren't in his office.

"Daniel, can you come here so I can talk with you please?"

"Not now, Jamie!" he hollers from down the hall. Yep, he's definitely in his office.

"Please?" I insist. I don't want dinner getting cold.

"What is it?" he asks as he walks toward the dining room. I step out into the hall to meet him, preventing him from seeing the spread Mylow and I made.

I lean in to kiss his cheek. "I know I've been giving you a hard time about not going back to school and about you not being here enough, and I'm sorry, so sorry, for that. I know you care about me and want me to be happy. I appreciate everything you've done for me and my family." I reach out and hold his hand. "I love you so much."

He looks almost flustered as I look up into his eyes. "Jamie, I don't know where this is coming from, but I like it. You're beginning to understanding. That's a good girl."

"Yes, I'm learning the hard way," I say just before he kisses me gently. He pulls back and smiles down at me.

179

"So, Mylow tells me that you have something special planned for me tonight?" he asks.

"Yes, let's go in here so you can see it for yourself." I take him by the hand and lead him into the dining room.

"Damn, girl! Did you do all this?"

I nod, smiling. "Yes, I did. Well, Mylow helped."

"I didn't know you had this in you," he says, grinning. I haven't seen a smile that big cross his face since the day I agreed to move in.

"It's so good to see you smiling, Daniel. I hope you enjoy it. If it tastes bad, you don't have to eat it. Not that it should! I'm pretty sure you'll enjoy my cooking."

"Anything that smells this great will taste just fine. I'm proud of you, woman! You truly surprised me tonight. I was upset, but you took all of that away."

I can't help but flush under his praise. He serves himself some food, fills Mylow's plate, and then fills mine as well. I pour wine for the men and tea for myself. Mylow enters and takes the seat to Daniel's right, while I sit at his left.

Christmas Eve has come sooner than I expect, though I'm not sure how. I've planned the perfect surprise for Daniel. I asked Mylow to gather every family picture of Daniel's family that he could find. I was shocked to see well over one hundred different images. I worked with a video company to create a video collage he can keep forever. It was so magical to finally see his family. I hope it means a lot to him when he sees them on the screen. I'm so nervous. I hope he likes it. I can't buy him anything he doesn't already have. He has designer clothes, shoes, watches—everything he could ever need. I wanted to give him something he would never forget. I can't wait to show him the video.

I'm feeling happier than I thought I would, but this is the first Christmas I've ever been away from my family. It's definitely harder than I thought it would be, but the joy of knowing Mama's being cared for helps, even though I haven't had the chance to call Ms. Marie back yet. I pray Mama is doing well. She loved to cook for us, especially on Christmas. We would sit down at the table as a family and love on each other. Daddy always had something special to give each of us. Every Christmas, he made us give away something special that we didn't need any more to the church for those less fortunate than ourselves. He urged us to give up something we still wanted to keep for ourselves because then we weren't just giving up old, tired toys and games. He called it sacrificing for others. I wasn't happy about it as a child, but looking back I can see what he meant for us to learn.

I wasn't able to send Mama a gift. I miss her—the old her—so much. I miss Daddy and Kelsie too. Maybe Daniel will let me call them so I can wish them a Merry Christmas. I love this time of year. The holidays always make me feel warm and happy inside, and I'm hoping this year stays the same, especially since Daniel is home. At least for a few days, I have him all to myself. I love him so much. I can't wait to see the look on his face when I show him his gift tomorrow.

Christmas morning started out very early for me. I couldn't sleep in, as usual. I guess I was too excited. But Daniel and Mylow slept in and once they were up, we agreed to exchange gifts after dinner. I've been keeping myself busy all day, but I can't wait much longer. We're just about to sit down to eat. I set up his video in the family room and I hope he enjoys it.

I'm so nervous. I think I'm going to slip upstairs really quick to change into something a little fancier for dinner. I want to look my best. I hurry up the stairs and throw open the closet. I flick through all my clothes and select the prettiest red dress that I can find. It looks amazing against my skin, so bright and vibrant. I know he'll love it on me. I've been working to get everything just right all day.

"Jamie, come on downstairs, pretty lady. It's time for dinner!"

It's time. Thank you, God, for such an amazing man. I rush downstairs and kiss him before heading into the dining room.

He usher me to place at the table and pull out my seat for me like a gentleman. I take my seat and watch him walk over to his seat. He is looking handsome as ever. We eat dinner alone Mylow is in his room. We talk briefly, but

I can't stop thinking about the video collage. I can't wait I haven't been able to give this man anything he doesn't already have. This is my chance to show him how much I love and care for him.

"So what is this Christmas present you've been trying to hide from me?"

"Who me? I would never hide anything from you—I can't anyway because you know everything."

"I hate surprises Jamie but I'll make an exception this time."

I get up to clear the table and tell Daniel to give me a few minutes to set things in place. I hurry to Mylow's room to get him to join us for the video. He agreed and followed me back into the family room where I asked Daniel to sit on the couch and relax. Daniel seems anxious but excited he wasn't sure what to expect. He watched me move about the room. I explained how much time I spent on making the video memorable as possible and that it took me a lot of time to plan without him finding out. I was nervous but excited to see his reaction. As the video started it begin with him as a baby which was labeled "the beginning". Then it displayed a few childhood memories with pictures of him playing around his parent's home. The next chapter was his middle school sporting moments with his team pictures—his parents were there every step of the way. As the video continued I saw Daniel's mood change quickly. He went from shocked to sad to emotionless. I wasn't sure how to read him. The video played on I showed his graduation from high school and him starting college before deciding to leave for the military. When the video reached the later years of his parent's before his mother took sick I could see it was bothering him. I could see he was very uncomfortable. I looked at Mylow for a quick answer on what to do wither to stop the video. But, before I could— Daniel got up swiftly in anger and knocked over everything in his way the glasses on the table, the vase, a chair he grabbed his coat and keys left out the door slamming it behind him. I was so shocked and scared I couldn't move Mylow looked at me in disbelief and said, "Jamie I'm sorry", and left out the door after Daniel.

∞∞∞

I can't believe it. I'm a mess. I've got tears everywhere. How was I supposed to know he would react like this? I thought the video dedication was something he would love, but he was so upset. I've never seen him like that before. He just got up from the table, glaring at me like he never wanted to see me again, and left the house. I offended him, I guess. I'm not sure how. I mean, maybe I should have warned him, but the man who made the video said that people do this all the time for their friends and spouses who have lost loved ones. Plus, Mylow was more surprised by his reaction than I was. I guess I don't really know Daniel. I feel so awful to have caused him so much pain. I hope he comes back tonight. I just can't seem to get this relationship right. I'm always wrong.

It's now two in the morning and he hasn't returned. I keep looking out the window, hoping I'll see his car in the driveway, hoping he comes home. I'm so tired right now. I can't believe I upset him so much. I hope he's okay. Mylow went to bed already and didn't seem to be too worried, but I can't rest knowing he was so upset.

What time is it now? I guess I must have drifted off. I sit up and look around—I'm in the bedroom. How did I get here? I could have sworn I fell asleep downstairs on the couch. Yeah, the last thing I remember was waiting for him to come home and watching the driveway.

Daniel's not in bed with me and he's not in the bathroom. Maybe Mylow woke up to get a glass of water and moved me? No, he wouldn't have. He would've just gotten me a blanket, I think. I crawl out of bed quietly and head down the hall to check the guest-room.

Before I can make it out the door, I trip over something on the floor—a small gift box and card. I flip open the card to see who the present is for—oh, its Daniel's present for me. I didn't see this before. He must have left this for me while I was asleep. Wow! It's a necklace with matching earrings. The necklace has my initials carved on the back of a huge diamond pendant. He's too much! Oh, now I feel even worse about my gift to him. I walk down the hall to the guest-room, hoping he's still awake.

I open the door just a crack and peer through. Daniel's lying on the bed asleep, still dressed in his clothing from earlier. Well, at least he's home. I step inside, wondering if he would be angry if I crawled in with him. I don't want to end my Christmas in anger. Well, I don't think he'll mind if I give him a quick kiss and thank him.

I approach him slowly and lean in to kiss his forehead, knowing nothing short of an alarm going off or the sun rising will wake him. "Daniel," I whispered, "I know you're sleeping but I just wanted to thank you for the lovely gift. I'm sorry your Christmas gift wasn't as nice."

Wait, what's that smell? I lean in close to him again. Is it women's perfume? It's all over him. I pick up his suit jacket from the floor. Huh, he must have been really tired—he never leaves his suits on the floor. I stand up, intending to drape it across the chair, but something falls out of one of his pockets. I reach down to grab it off the floor and feel...cloth? Silk? It's not his tie; he still has that on. What is this? I hold it up to the moonlight streaming through the open window and it's a pair of women's panties.

I can't believe this. He was out all night with a woman—on Christmas! What kind of hussy is out on Christmas and loses her panties? Why did he keep them? Did he really rush out of here, all upset, and then dive into another woman's arms? I stuff the panties back into his suit jacket pocket and leave, shutting the door behind myself.

What was I thinking waiting up for him? How long has this been going on? All those nights away from me, was he with her? I can't help my cries from escaping. I try to hold them back, but soon I'm sobbing. I rush into the bathroom so I don't wake him. I turn on the shower and climb in, my wet drenched in the warm water as it cascades over me.

How could I think I was enough for this man? I'm just some girl he picked up off the street—literally. I wonder what she looks like. Is she prettier than me? She must be. What does he see in her that he doesn't see in me? I can't believe how much this hurts. It feels like I'm dying inside, crushed and crumbled. I haven't felt anything like this since Daddy died. It's like I'm losing Daniel. I can't even try to explain how defeated and hurt I feel. I can't help but think if I hadn't gone looking for him, if I'd stayed out of the guest-room, I wouldn't have ever found that. But, no, that's wrong. I needed to know. I can't imagine this having gone on any longer and me not knowing about it.

∞∞∞

February 1993

It's been quiet around here for the past month. I wrote a little this morning. It helped me get my head around my feelings some. I ended up with a poem I entitled "Meant for Love". I feel a little bit better, a bit lighter now, like the poem was a release.

Mylow is gone for the day. Daniel's here, but he's sleeping. He came in really late again as he has more often these days. I know he'll be asleep for a few more hours at least. I want to go into the office. For the past month, I've been dying to see if I can find a picture or anything about this woman. I need to know who she is and how long this has been going on. I know I shouldn't do this, but I must know. I can't have this just sitting in the back of my mind all the time. I have at least a thirty-minute window to get in and out of there before Daniel wakes up.

I head down into his office and quietly open the door. I leave it open behind me so I can hear if he wakes up. Hopefully, I'd be able to put back whatever I found and make it out of the office before he made it downstairs. I'm pretty sure I can. He normally wakes up and heads straight for the shower. I should have plenty of time.

Daniel would kill me if he knew what I was doing right now, but I have to find something. I wish I didn't have to invade his privacy to do it, but he's cheating and I need to know more before I can confront him. Maybe this is why he doesn't want me in here. Maybe he has more secrets he wants to hide than just a woman on the side.

I start at his bookcase and start going through the books, one by one. I ignore the small ones, too easy to find something hidden in them and stick to the larger ones. There are so many different kinds of books. Oh, what's this? It doesn't feel like a normal book.

I pull it off the shelf—it's an encyclopedia. Huh. I flip it open, but it opens like a small box. I pause and listen closely to the upstairs—no sound whatsoever. I quickly rifle through what's inside. Photo IDs? Papers with a ton of different numbers? Cards? What is all this? Who are these people? None of this means anything to me? What's Daniel hiding? This isn't what I wanted to find. Maybe this is for his work? I have no idea. I put everything back into the box and put the fake encyclopedia back on the bookshelf exactly where it was. There has to be something about her in here somewhere. I'm running out of time. I listen for him again before opening up his desk and carefully going through everything, being extra cautious to put it all back where I found it.

"You have to be in here somewhere, lady. Now, where are you?" I mutter to myself. "Maybe an address? Phone number? Come on," I continue as I check through his pen and pencil drawer. There's nothing, not even a Post-It note. She's so important that he spends his nights with her and takes her to fancy dinners when I'm stuck here alone, but there's nothing about her anywhere? Maybe she's his wife—oh no. *Maybe she's his wife!* What if I'm the other woman? What if they have a family living in the condo and I'm here. No, why would you have a family in the condo and not the big family house? Oh, who knows! Rich people do crazy things. What's this? There's something stuck under this drawer.

I twist my wrist and my nail manages to catch the false bottom of the drawer and drag it out. It's mostly a bunch of financial files, but there's a picture too. I flip to it and turn it over. Oh good God in Heaven! Who is this man? Why is he dead? Why would Daniel have a picture of a man lying dead on the ground, riddled with bullet wounds, in his desk like this?

No.

No. No. No. He didn't do this. There's no way Daniel did this or had any hand it in.

I carefully put the files and the photo back into the drawer; replace the false bottom and the things that went on top of it before rushing out of the room.

It's been hours and I can't get that picture out of my mind. I pace back and forth across the bedroom, just trying to keep myself together.

The man was on the ground dead. Oh God, why? I need to keep it together! How can I go on like I didn't see that? Who were those people on the IDs? Are they all dead? I didn't see the man, but I wasn't looking for him either. Oh, Daniel, what did you do?

"Jamie?" Daniel calls from the guest-room.

"Yes, Daniel?" I call out as I stop pacing. "I'm in here! I'm trying to find a stud I dropped in the closet." I hastily wipe my eyes and quietly open the closet and drop to a crouch. Daniel comes in a moment later. "You finally got out of bed I see."

"It was a long night," he says.

"I bet it was."

"I saw you in bed, so I didn't want to wake you."

"Actually, I feel asleep on the couch last night, waiting for you to return. Thank you for helping me to bed."

"I didn't see you on the couch. You were asleep in bed when I came home. Are you sure you fell asleep down stairs?"

"Yes, I do from time to time when I'm waiting for you. Mylow always says what days you'll be home, but he never knows the exact time. I know it's late sometimes, but I like waiting up for you. I like welcoming you home," I say.

I've been waiting up trying to catch a whiff of her perfume on him when he gets home. I keep holding out hope that it was just that one time, just because he was upset.

"Jamie, I've wanted to talk to you about how I acted after you gave me the video for Christmas." I nod and he continues, "I was dealing with some things at the time. I never told you, but it brought back memories that I haven't faced in years. I appreciate what you did. It was very thoughtful. I wasn't upset with you, just upset at having to remember. I have a lot going on and it was a reminder of how I failed my parents. I want to make it up to you."

"Daniel, that was months ago. Don't worry about it."

"I don't want to forget about it. I want to take you to see a movie—your choice this time. How does that sound?" he asks.

I smile stiffly. "It sounds great. Thank you."

"Be ready by six. We'll head to the theater then. I'm going downstairs to the office to take care of some business before we go. Mylow will return tomorrow evening. He's spending time with his family."

"Family?" I'm shocked. Mylow has a family? "I never heard him talk about a family," I say, dumbfounded. "Well, I guess he doesn't talk a lot about anything, really."

"It's complicated, Jamie. It's his private business. Don't butt in."

"I understand. I get it. Sorry." He nods and pulls me into his arms.

"So, it's just me and you tonight, pretty lady."

Our night out was amazing. We weren't far from home. They have so many nice places nearby. It was just like when we were dating. He courted me and was such a gentleman. When we got home, I forgot, just for a moment, what I found in his office and even about the panties I found on Christmas. Daniel was so affectionate and attentive. He is a man of many talents. He's so passionate.

When we were making love, he was so caught up in the moment that he didn't stop this time to use protection. I didn't realize until it was too late. He knows I'm not on any type of birth control. I won't worry about it.

After we made love, he pulled me close and said, "Jaime, I don't know what I would do without you in my life." He sounded so truthful, but I'm not sure I can believe him, not after what I found.

∞∞∞∞

Spring 1993

I keep finding myself day dreaming, thinking about the man's face from the picture. I can see him so clearly in my mind. What happened to him? What's Daniel involved in? There's definitely no way Daniel can know I was in his office. I can't chance him finding out that I know. There's no telling what he would do to me. I wish I didn't need to go back in there again, but I have to call Ms. Marie to get an update on Mama. I told her I would call, but I didn't think it would take me this long. That's not the only reason, though. I want to understand what's going on around me too.

It's been a few months now since I was last able to get in there. Daniel's been in and out like normal, but Mylow's been around constantly. But, this morning Mylow is picking Daniel up from the airport. It's a little peculiar. Mylow hardly ever picks him up—he usually just sends a car service or Daniel drives himself, if he drove there. It doesn't matter, though. I'm getting in that office one way or another. I'll have at least an hour to work with this time.

I've been waiting patiently all morning for Mylow to leave. Then, just when he does, Ms. Janice comes over early. I had to wait for her to go upstairs and start cleaning; I didn't want her to think anything weird was going on. I think this will be my only shot.

I've been puttering around in the kitchen, baking up some of Daniel's favorite cookies while I wait. Now that they've both cleared out, I can head into the office. I hesitate just as I reach for the knob, but I can hear the vacuum running upstairs, which means she still has a ways to go. There are two bathrooms and a bunch of rooms to clean and tidy. I open the door and realize that I don't have a plan. Where do I start? I bring my thumb to my mouth, about to nibble on my nail. Wow, my nerves are fried. I haven't wanted to do that in ages. I drop my hand to my side and think.

Maybe I'll write down the names of the people on the IDs. Hopefully I'll find a name for the man on the picture; any information would help. But help what? I just want to take another look at him first.

I go to the drawer and try to tug it open—it's locked. It wasn't locked before. Was that a mistake or does he know I'd been in there? Maybe he's just got something worse in there now. I don't have time for this. *Okay, think Jaime, think!* Where else might I find information? I'm not

194

even sure what I want it for, just that I know it'll be helpful.

His filing cabinet! I can always hear him rustling around in there. I quietly tug open the drawers, knowing how loud they can be, and flip through his manila folders. Huh.

What's this? The file has my initials on it? I pull it out and quickly listen—vacuum still running and I didn't hear the garage. I open the file—oh my God. Why does he have them? Where did he get them? There are pictures of me walking on campus, getting off the bus, even pictures of me walking into my house. There's pictures of the church and, oh my! Pictures of Jace and me walking into the church together. There are even some of my classmates and people in the study group I went to once or twice. I can't believe him! This picture of Jace and me walking into the church! I think that was one of the first times I volunteered! Wait a minute—he knew where I was the night he called! He knew I was with Jace. Why did he have me followed? He never asked me about Jace. What is going on here?

I flip through more photos of campus and the church and all the people I met and stumble on one of a bright, sunny street lined with palm trees. Where is this? I flip through a couple more and find Kelsie. I can't believe him. She must be in California. Her hair is different and she looks so pretty and happy. But, some of these pictures—the ones on campus, especially—date back to before I met him. What the hell was Daniel doing? Why was he having me followed? I've never done a wrong thing in my life. I'm not rich or well connected. I don't have anything he might have wanted. Well, it doesn't matter now. I need to get it together and call Ms. Marie to check on Mama. I might not have a chance for a long while. I tuck everything away back where I found it, making sure nothing looks even the slightest bit out of place.

Then, I grab the receiver and dial her number. She answers on the second ring. "Hello?"

"Hi, Ms. Marie. This is Jamie calling you back for Mama's number. I'm sorry it took me so long to get back to you. Things here have been hectic."

"Oh, hello there, baby girl. Well, your mama is going home this weekend. It took a little longer than expected, but she's so happy about everything and is doing fine."

"I'm so glad to hear that. Has she seen the house?"

"No, I don't think so. From what I heard, they wanted to surprise her this weekend. Everyone is meeting in front of the house to celebrate. You know, your father worked hard for that house. He was a good man. He did a lot of stuff for people on this street and in this neighborhood. We never did anything to show our appreciation for him when he was alive or after he passed on. I think we all feel a little guilty for that, but now we can honor him and your mother in a special way. I hate that you can't be here to see the look on your mama's face when she see her new house."

"Me too, Ms. Marie. Oh, do you know if she ever found out who donated the money?"

"She sure did, honey! It was a nice young man from the church that's not too far from here. He was coming by regularly to check on her and bringing her stuff all time. He's just an angel. That's what she calls him—her angel. He worked with a couple of companies and got them to donate time, skills, and materials and, oh honey, I'm not sure. He worked it all out though. In the end, she got a completely new fixed up house. Just like your daddy always wanted."

Nice boy from the church? No, it can't be. "Ms. Marie by chance was his name Jace?"

"I believe so, Jamie. That sounds about right. Yeah, I think that is his name." I can't breathe. I can barely think. It was Jace who did all that? Not Daniel? Has Daniel done anything? "Are you there, honey? You got quiet."

"Yes, ma'am. I'm sorry, but I have to go now," I say, trying to keep my voice calm and level. I'm not very successful.

"Are you okay, Jamie?"

"Yes, ma'am. I'm just so happy for her. Thank you for keeping me updated. I'll call Mama next week when she gets home. Please let me surprise her."

"Okay, I will. You take care of yourself."

197

"I will. Thank you, Ms. Marie."

I hang up the phone and take a deep breath. I can't believe what I just heard.

"Who's there?" someone calls from the hallway. I jump before I recognize the voice as Ms. Janice's.

"Oh, it's just me, Ms. Janice," I say as I walk out into the hall, closing the door behind me. I think I left everything where I found it. "I was just in here looking for a picture of Daniel really quickly. I'm having a painting made of him and the artist needs a reference. It's a surprise," I say trying to come up with a decent reason as quickly as possible.

"Oh, okay, Ms. Jamie," she says. I don't think she believes me, though.

"Ms. Janice, please don't say anything about me being in here to Daniel or Mylow. Please? I don't want to ruin the surprise or upset Daniel. You know how he is about this office," I say, smiling sheepishly as I shrug. I should have gone to acting school; I'm so good at this.

"I won't. That's your business, not mine."

"Thank you so much," I say, letting relief color my tone. "I'm going to my room now to rest—unless you're not done up there? I don't want to be in your way."

"Oh, no. I'm done upstairs. Are you feeling well? You look really tired, Ms. Jamie."

"Yes, ma'am. I'm doing fine. I just need to lie down a while, I think. Thanks for asking."

She nods and heads into the kitchen to clean. I jog upstairs quickly. I practically run into the bedroom and throw myself onto the bed, burying my face in my pillow.

I can't believe all of this time I thought he was a good person, so caring and giving. He's been playing me since the beginning. He hunted me down like an animal, spying on me and watching me. He picked me out like I was a piece of furniture. He had me followed. He knew about my friendship with Jace and never said a word. Why would he do that? What did he gain? He knew when I was with him at the church. He deceived me.

I mean, my volunteer work and friendship with Jace weren't secrets, but I never bothered to really talk about it either. I was always too wrapped up in Daniel to talk about Jace or the church while I was with him.

Who is this monster I'm living with? I can't believe I fell right into his hands. I was such easy prey for him. He needed to make his situation believable for the people he was trying to impress. I think he wanted someone to warm his bed and I was convenient. Someone innocent and unaware of all the bad things he was doing. Someone who wouldn't question his authority. He's sick and twisted. I must have seemed so simple to him. I just gave him whatever he wanted. He doesn't care about my mother or me. He never intended to take care of her. He said and did whatever he had to so I would believe him and listen to him. I feel so sick and disgusted. Nausea rushes through me as someone knocks on my door.

"Jamie, are you in there? Jamie…" Daniel says. I didn't hear the front door, or the sound of Daniel calling for me. Which, judging by his tone, he'd been doing for a while.

"Yes," I say, trying to sound sleepy.

I was just checking on you. I missed you. I'm coming in."

"Wait—" I say, scrambling for a reason to ask him not to come into his own bedroom.

Daniel ignores my small protest. "No, you're fine, pretty lady. You look good just like you are."

"I've been thinking about you non-stop for the last few hours," I say, trying to keep my tone normal, happy.

"Really, what did I do to deserve that?" he asks as he sits down next to me.

"Just being yourself," I say.

"Are you feeling okay?" he asks. "Ms. Janice said you came up here earlier."

Why is he so concerned all of a sudden? Why is he asking all of these questions now? How dare he ask like he has a right to be worried when he's never even home.

"I know. I haven't been sleeping well. I'm just tired," I insist.

"Well, you do look tired. But, come on down. I have dinner waiting for us." He never asks, does he? He's always telling me what to do. It's infuriating.

"I'm not that hungry," I say. "I'd rather just get some rest tonight."

Daniel's face sets, firm. "Come down. I need your company."

I sigh quietly, not wanting to anger him. "Give me a few minutes, please." I guess I should jump and get right to it. I don't want to end up like that man on the picture, I think.

Daniel grumbles and leaves the room. I can hear him stomping down the stairs like a spoiled child.

After about five minutes, I drag myself out of bed. I fix my hair and straighten my clothes before heading back down. I get to the table and settle into my seat, waiting for him to fix me a plate like he always does. He likes to dish out my servings to make sure I'm eating healthy. Part of me thinks it's about making sure I'm not going to get fat. This man, he's nothing like I thought he was. After about five minutes at the table, he starts talking—all charm and persuasion. What a fake.

"Jamie, I wanted to talk with you about your future. I know you wanted to go back to school, but I'm thinking we need something more than that."

More than an education? What is he talking about? "What do you mean, Daniel?" I ask.

"I've decided we need to start a family. I need to bring something into my life that adds real meaning, real purpose. I think a child will do that."

"A child? Now?" I ask, struggling to keep my disgust and revulsion out of my tone.

"Yes, now. I think this is what's best for us, best for your future."

Best for my future? Who is he kidding? When I haven't finished college? I'm too young right now. Let alone the fact that he's telling, not asking if I want children. He's telling me we're going to have them. What am I going to do? He never stopped to ask me what I think because whatever he wants he gets.

"Are you sure? Children are a lot of work and you're not home very often, Daniel."

"You're strong. I'm sure you can handle it. I mean, what else do you do all day?"

I nod, unable to speak my mind. I want to say, "Well, I would be in school if you'd let me have the money for it or just tell Mylow to take me," but I don't want to end up like the man in the photo.

Every bit of food that enters my mouth tastes like dirt. I don't want to eat it, but I can't just leave the table without having eaten. I quickly finish my plate and make my excuses to go back upstairs, saying I have a headache.

I shed my clothing and crawl into bed wearing the comfiest pajamas I have. I would rather die than have a child with him. I'll never be okay with having a baby with him. Not after everything that I've found. He's full of lies and deceit. I'm still trying to figure out who he really is behind closed doors. This baby talk is crazy and reckless. Even if I hadn't found those things, I don't think we'd be ready for children. We're not even married. I almost said that at the table, but I didn't want to encourage him. I don't know how I would get out of planning a wedding. As he said, it's not like I have anything else to do.

I need to find a way to get out of here. But, when it's all said and done, I have no power at all. And, the truth is, I feel like I can't say no to him. I'm afraid of what he'll do if I say anything against what he thinks. I'm too terrified to even ask him to use protection. Eventually, I'll end up pregnant. I don't want this! I just don't!

Loneliness Within

Confusion

The day is lonely,
The nights are long,
Trying to figure out exactly what went wrong
You speak of your heart being true,
But your actions show lies that simply describe you
An enormous price one pays to love
We were put here,
To serve a purpose,
To understand,
God's plan as a man and a woman should
Loving through all of the hurt,
And trials, like no one else could
The reward for love is to reap happiness,
Instead, the price one pays for pain is long-suffering,
Confusion.
Confused about the truth,
Confused about the facts,
Which part was just added
And which part truth lacks,
No one would choose to be tangled up in such *loneliness*,
Or simply to lose.

Chapter Thirteen

Early 1994

Over the last few months, all I can think about is finding a way to leave here safely. The days are flying by and I'm merely a passenger in my own life. I don't know when I'll leave or how—all I know is I have to get away. I can't be a part of whatever he's doing. I have a very sick feeling something bad is going on. Mylow hasn't been talking as much to me these days. I mean, he wasn't ever a chatterbox, but he's always been good for a light conversation while I'm cooking or baking or listening to the radio.

I don't sleep much anymore. Since Daniel brought up having children, my nightmares have only gotten worse. I keep dreaming about the faces on the IDs and the more I think about the list of numbers, the more I think they're bank accounts. Maybe the accounts are linked to those people on the IDs?

Loneliness Within

I sit down heavily on the living room sofa and hang my head in my hands. What am I doing here? He's never given me a good reason for why I can't see Mama. I wonder why that is? He could have said almost anything. Instead, everything is a secret. Everything's for my protection. Protection against what? I'm like a prisoner living in a beautifully designed prison cell. Sure, I can have anything I want, but I can't leave. I'm trapped and if Daniel had it his way, I would be barefoot and pregnant, like a good little housewife. I was so foolish! I can't believe I thought this man was my Prince Charming, the love of my life. I hung on his every word. It hurts to see how naïve I was, how desperate I must have been not to see his true self.

Ms. Janice is my only connection to the outside world. I'm terrified of losing her. The other day I asked her for a favor—a huge one. She agreed to secretly mail off letters to Mama for me; in exchange, I'll pay her for her silence. She's playing a dangerous game and I didn't want to cost her job if Daniel finds out.

In my letter to Mama, I gave her pieces of information for her to hang onto for me. I told her only so much, but it's hidden inside the paragraphs so it won't seem so obvious—like the names of the folks from the IDs. I explained they were friends of mine I wanted her to know about. I also asked her save the number sequence—that they meant something and I'd discuss it with her later. I have to give her bits at a time and not all at once. Otherwise, I'm worried she'll panic even though I told her that she shouldn't. I told her I'm okay, but that I just need her to store some information for me in secret. I asked her not to talk to anyone about it, especially not Steve. He could be in on this too for all I know. If there's anything I've realized lately, it's how little I know about what's going on. I don't want to take any chances.

I wish I could say more to Mama. I have so much I'd like to tell her, but too much could scare her into acting prematurely, which could get us all killed. I asked her not to try to contact me right now and I didn't put my address on the letters just in case. She's a stubborn woman, which should help me too. If I don't give it to her willingly, she's not going to ask. I'll go back into the office and get some more evidence as soon as I can. I'll keep sending her stuff until I feel she has enough to go to the police with. I can't waste any time. I have to get as much evidence as I can, as quickly as I can. They can investigate the people on the IDs and find out if they've been reported missing or if they're alive and well. Maybe they can find out what happened to that man in the picture.

I won't rest until I'm free from this place. I hope it's not too late for those people.

∞∞∞

May 1994

Ms. Janice mailed Mama a third letter for me. I gave her more money. She didn't want to take it, but I forced her to. I want her to know this is too important to me and the money doesn't matter. I told her to buy her kids something special with it or to save it in case she gets caught. I need her discretion. I can't have Mylow finding out about what I'm doing. It wouldn't be fair to Ms. Janice or Mama to have my poor choices cause them harm. I've been so anxious and nervous lately. This is all I can think about. I've been eavesdropping on Daniel and Mylow's conversations whenever I can without chancing getting caught. I need to get back into the office, but this week they've both been home all the time.

Not sleeping is definitely beginning to wear me down. I'm constantly tired and I haven't been feeling well. I think I must be coming down with something. I can't get the letters and the evidence they hold out of my mine. I sure hope Mama's getting them and not Steve. That would be devastating. I'd probably be back at square one if that's what's happening.

The past few days have been a struggle just to get out of bed. I need to go back in the office, but I feel too weak to get up. Every time I smell food or move too fast, I get nauseous. Even Daniel's cologne that I once loved now makes my stomach revolt. This flu is not fun at all. Daniel's heading out of town tonight and he made Mylow promise to call his physician in the morning if I'm not feeling better. He said the doctor would come by for a house call. Daniel said not to bother him with the news of how I am unless it's something serious. Apparently, business is more important than me.

∞∞∞∞

I woke up this morning and didn't feel any better. Mylow called the doctor not too long ago. I have no desire to eat, but he keeps trying to feed me. Everything that goes down, comes right back up. He even got Ms. Janice to help. She brought me some of her homemade chicken soup. It's the only thing that's stayed down at all and I can only take sips of it. I'm too tired to keep more down. My fever isn't very high. If I didn't feel so poorly, I wouldn't think I had one at all. Part of me hopes Daniel gets this flu too, but mostly I wouldn't wish this on anyone.

I can't look at Mylow the same these days. He knows what's going on around here. He's a part of all of it, which makes him as cold and heartless as Daniel. I'll never trust him again. I can't trust anyone, but I do think I need a doctor. Mylow said I looked pale, which I think is a nice way of saying I look like death. I know I'm losing weight. It's this house, these walls, and the evil that lurks in that office. The more I'm here, the more I know, the more I hate to be here. Maybe I'm dying.

I close my eyes one minute and wake up three hours later to an older man hovering over me. I can't quite make out what he's saying at first.

"I'm here to evaluate you."

"Huh?" I ask. He must be the doctor.

"I'm Doctor Brown, Ms. Jamie. Mylow tells me you've been feeling weak lately? That you've been staying in bed without an appetite? He also said something about a low fever, which I see you do have—99.8 degrees Fahrenheit."

"Yes, sir," I mumble. "I can't raise my head for long and I'm cold most of the time. I feel nauseous all the time too."

"I'm going to take some blood samples and see what's going on, okay? I'll have them sent to the lab, but there are some quicker tests I'd like to run. If you don't mind, can the nice Ms. Janice help you to the restroom? I'd like to get a urine sample."

I nod, unable to speak.

The doctor waves Ms. Janice in and she helps me onto the toilet and leaves me to my privacy. I give the doctor the sample and he takes out a couple of little paper sticks to dip into the cup. After a few minutes, he mutters to himself. When I look at him questioningly, he just smiles and says he'll know for sure after the blood tests come back. He tells me I'm dangerously dehydrated, which is causing my lightheadedness and says that I'll feel quite a bit better after solving that. He prescribes me a special drink to help replace my electrolytes and gives Mylow a couple of other prescriptions for me too, including a strong anti-nausea medication. I thank the doctor and he leaves. Mylow shows him out and then returns to my side.

"What can I get for you, Ms. Jamie? I'm really worried about you. I think I'm going to call Daniel."

"No, please don't. He said before he didn't want to be bothered unless it was an emergency. The doctor says I'll be fine with some medications and something to hydrate me. This is just a bug; I'll be fine. I'll take the medicines and drink plenty of water and the electrolyte drink he prescribed. Let's wait for the tests to come back, at least, okay?" I ask him, trying to be rational. "I don't want to worry him for nothing."

Mylow sighs and nods. "Okay, I'll only agree to this if you promise to tell me if you feel worse so I can get you to the hospital."

"Yes, I promise."

"All right. Then I'm going to run to the pharmacy and fill these for you, okay? I'll be back in half an hour. Ms. Janice has agreed to stay with you."

I turn to Ms. Janice. "Oh, you don't have to do that. I don't want you to be late picking up your kids."

"Their aunt picked them up for me. Don't worry, Ms. Jamie."

Over the next two days, even with the anti-nausea medication and the increased fluids, I feel significantly worse and I keep throwing up. Worried, Mylow calls the doctor on his cell phone and puts him on speakerphone so I don't have to hold it to my ear, and, I suspect, so I don't hide anything from him.

"Hi Doctor Brown," I say weakly.

How do you feel, today? Mylow says you're feeling worse?"

"I'm not sure. I might be the same, but I'm definitely not any better. I'm really tired. I feel weaker than before. I think my head hurts more."

"Well, Ms. Jamie, I'm not surprised, sadly. Many women in your condition end up in the hospital at least a couple of times. I ran several tests and I believe you have hyperemesis gravidarum, or HG for short."

"Hyper-what? What's HG?" I ask, becoming increasingly concerned.

"It's nothing too bad. It's something a small percentage of pregnant women get. In layman's terms, it's the worst morning sickness possible. Many women with HG are hospitalized for dehydration at one point or another."

"I don't have the flu?" Then it hits me. Pregnant. I'm stunned. I couldn't remember missing a period, but at this point I'm not sure I would have noticed. I've been so stressed about the letters and collecting evidence. "I'm sorry, doctor. Did you say I'm pregnant?"

Mylow's mouth drops open.

"You heard right. You're pregnant. From the hCG levels, I'd say about 6-8 weeks. As the medications haven't helped your HG, I'm going to have Mylow bring you to the hospital. I've already spoken to him about it. You need IV fluids and to be monitored if we're to keep you and the baby healthy. After you stabilize, we can talk long-term plans. I don't want to put you or your baby at risk."

I feel a sudden surge of anger and energy. "No! I won't go to the hospital not now."

"With how you're feeling and how you looked two days ago, you and the baby should be under 24-hour care. Mylow, my suggestion is to call Daniel and have him give me a call. I know this is a lot for you, Ms. Jamie, but the best thing for you and the baby is to get appropriate medical care."

Mylow and the doctor talk for a few more minutes, but I tune them out. I can't handle any of this right now. Soon, Mylow hangs up and calls Daniel, who immediately says he's on his way home and tells Mylow to take me to the nearest, best hospital.

I barely remember getting into the car. The car ride is making me feel extra nauseous. I didn't know that was possible at this point. I pray silently: *God, if you can hear me, I'm so sorry for making bad life choices. I'm sorry that I haven't talked to you in so long. I'm not sure I even know what to say anymore, but you know my heart. I don't want this baby, not now and definitely not from this man. I hate the idea of being pregnant. I know it's not the baby's fault, but I'd never be able to love it like it deserves, especially not here. I didn't have a say in any of this. This is wrong. I would never bring a baby into Daniel's sick and twisted life. I hate this so much. Help me, God! Please!*

I pray with everything I have until I fall asleep on the way to the hospital. When I wake up, Daniel is leaning over me, wiping my brow.

"Jamie? Jamie, how do you feel?"

"Not so good," I mumble.

"Pretty lady, you've been sleep since yesterday when Mylow checked you into the hospital. The doctor says you're extremely weak and that you still have a fever off and on. They're trying to make sure they didn't overlook anything because your condition normally doesn't come with a fever, but it might just be a little cold."

I nod, barely able to move my head. When I try to shift my arm, I feel a sick pulling. I turn slowly and look— I'm hooked up to several different IV bags. "Will the baby survive?" I'm not sure I want to know, but I have to ask.

"I hope so!" Daniel says. "There's a part of me growing inside of you. I'll do whatever it takes to make sure that baby survives, Jamie. I didn't realize what I was missing until I found out you were pregnant. It hit me all at once. I need this to work out, Jamie. Please try to rest and get better. I told the doctor not to let you leave this place until you're feeling 100%, okay? I don't care how much it costs. This is too important to me. I'll bring my work home as much as I can. I won't leave you. I'll be around more to help. I'll do anything for you, anything you need."

"Daniel, I'm sorry," I mumble, yawning. "I need to rest now, okay? Please understand. I want to talk, but I can't right now."

"Of course I understand, pretty lady. I'll go downstairs for a while. I'll be back to check on you later. Rest and please get better. Don't disappoint me now, okay?"

"Okay." Daniel kisses my forehead and rubs his hand over my lower belly. I almost throw up. I'm so happy he stopped touching me and left the room. I don't care that I'm in a hospital. I'm just thrilled to have his filthy hands off of me.

How can he make a complete change, just like that? For as long as I've been living with him, he's been distant and busy. And then, just like that, he can suddenly bring his work home and tend to my needs? This is the same man who sleeps alone most of the time and then, out the blue, wants a family. I can't believe that he can change like that. He's got to be up to something.

God please no. Daniel has a full life for us planned out now. At this point, I would rather be dead then stuck barefoot and pregnant. This isn't what I wanted. This isn't how I want my life to be. This isn't what I thought moving in with him would mean.

Someone knocks gently on the open door to my room. This room is secluded, which helps some. The person at the door is an older man dressed in a white lab coat.

"Jamie, I'm Doctor Raymond, your treating physician. I'm an HG and high-risk pregnancy specialist. I'm here to help you through this. How do you feel right now?"

"I'm tired, weak, and easily irritated."

The doctor chuckles. "We've done every reasonable test on you and we can't find anything wrong other than your HG and a possible minor infection, like a cold. So, with rest and fluids you should be better in a few days. When you go home, I'll have some stronger anti-nausea medications for you. While you're here, we're going to figure out what foods and drinks you can keep down best in order to maximize your nutritional and fluid intake. Tell me, do you plan on more children?"

"Why?" I ask.

"Women who experience HG during pregnancy often experience it for every pregnancy. Not always, but often. If you were intending on having more than one—"

"Not right now, no." The doctor nods.

I'll be back to check on you later tonight before the end of my shift. Is there anyone you would like for me to call?" He pauses, and then speaks carefully. "Anyone other than your husband? Sometimes family is all you need to get better." He's offering me an out, but I can't take it right now. I don't want to endanger anyone else.

"No, doctor, there is no one else. Thanks for asking." He nods.

The days blur together. I can't remember anything. Nothing they do stops my nausea and I can't keep anything down, not even water. Everything is hazy and confusing.

"Mrs. Lester can you hear me?" I think it's one of the doctors—the voice sounds far away and fuzzy.

Yes. I try to say it, but I can't make the word come out of my mouth. My tongue sticks to the roof of my mouth. I try again.

"Yes."

"Your fever has subsided, but you're still rejecting everything you try to eat or drink. I'm concerned about the health of you and your baby. You've lost an alarming amount of weight if what your husband said you weighed a month ago is accurate. If you're malnourished, then the baby may be too, given how much you've deteriorated in just a few days. I'll need to talk with your husband, but I think if we don't see a fast improvement, we may be looking at a feeding tube."

I don't understand. A feeding tube? "What?" I ask, trying to put as much as I can into simple words.

"We must get food to your body before you starve to death. Your husband says you weren't eating well before you started to feel ill, so it's quickly becoming our only option."

"No," I say harshly. "No tube." I take a deep breath and force out, "I'll never agree to a feeding tube."

The doctor frowns, concerned. "I'll let you think about it and I'll get back with you in a few hours to see what your final decision will be."

It's a blur between when the doctor leaves and when Daniel comes in. I think they're just minutes apart, but I think it's been hours.

"Jamie, the doctor is saying you need a tube to help get food to the baby and your body. I know you hate being in here. You're having a hard time, but think, Jamie, there's a precious little baby growing inside of you who's innocent. You have to take care of yourself. I won't allow you to say no and risk losing the baby."

Everything hurts and I can't go on anymore. I just want to go to sleep and not wake up again. I just want it to be over.

"Daniel," I say, struggling to get my words out. "I've never seen you so concerned about anyone or anything like this. I'm tired and I'm not going to fight you. Just do whatever you decide to do. I know I really don't have a say in the matter anyway."

Daniel grins. "I'm glad you understand it's not up for discussion."

The world goes dark again and a frantic, loud beeping briefly wakes me. I can vaguely make out Daniel shouting, "There's blood everywhere! Come, please!"

I gather my strength and look down at the red drenching through the sheets.

∞∞∞∞

This has been the worst week of my adult life. I feel awful. I've been in severe pain for days now. I'm thankful to be home from the hospital. I don't remember much of my final days there. I'm feeling so many things right now. I had a miscarriage. I went through an emergency procedure to stop the bleeding, but in the end, I completely lost the baby and they had to clean out my insides. I feel so raw and open and empty—like I've been scrubbed too hard, too much. I feel new and different, but I'm not sure I like it. It's very confusing. I feel completely different.

Did I do this? Did I will this to happen? Did I lose my baby on purpose? I know I didn't want the baby, but I didn't want to kill it either. What kind of person am I? I hated the thought of having a baby with Daniel. I even asked God to take it from me.

I guess he did.

Did that innocent baby suffer because of me? Was the baby already sick or hurt from my illness? I hate myself. I thought this was what I wanted. I wasn't ready to be a mother and now I'm not anymore. Oh God! What have I done?

∞∞∞

January 1995

Another year has come and gone. Christmas was quiet; Daniel spent the day sleeping in his room. The weeks are passing by slowly. No one says much to me these days. Ms. Janice came in and said hello the first couple times she was working after the miscarriage, but I heard Daniel pull her aside a few weeks ago and tell her that I needed my privacy and wasn't to be bothered. He reminded her again that her job is to clean the house and for her to focus on that. He cut off our friendship. I have no one to talk to now. I sit in silence most of the time, letting it suck the life out of me. I can feel the house eating me alive, just small pieces of my soul disappearing at a time. I think I'm going insane, but this is the price I must pay. I can't talk to anyone about how I'm feeling. Everything seems so cloudy and dark.

I'm in a real mess. I can't go on ignoring it. I cry all the time. I try not to look at myself in the mirror; I don't like what I see. I spend almost all of my time in bed, buried under the covers. Whenever I do look in the mirror, I see someone selfish, someone who wished for something to kill her baby.

I can't take this anymore. I don't know what to do. I sigh and stare at the ceiling.

God, I say quietly to myself. *I know you're up there, please help me. I'm dying inside. I can't fight myself anymore. I need to be closer to you. I want to know you for myself.*

I stop and stifle the sobs that begin to escape.

I don't know how to do this. I've made some bad decisions. Surely, this won't be how my life ends. I know there is more for me than this. I might be damaged goods, but I'm still me. I know I was pregnant and had a miscarriage, but who would want me after this?

I can't keep my thoughts straight. I don't know what to think. I take a deep breath before continuing my heartfelt prayer: *No one would want me because I wouldn't want me.*

"God of my father, please hear me. I'm sorry for everything I've done. I want to be free from here. Free from this internal pain and rejection I feel. Amen!

I'm determined to start over.

∞∞∞

When I wake up each morning, I try to convince myself to get up, to get going. It takes a while, but I manage it. It's a new day today and I get to start over again. I have to look at it like that. I decide to go downstairs and talk to Mylow. I don't care if he doesn't respond. I need to tell him how I feel. I want to tell him I'm sorry for putting him in so many difficult situations.

"Mylow, I want to talk to you please."

"Ms. Jamie, you're out of bed. Are you okay? What's going on?" he asks, a surprising amount of concern in his voice.

"You're a good person, deep down inside, Mylow. I know you are. I've been around here going out of my mind long enough. I know when I fall asleep on the couch you pick me up and put me to bed. You don't have to say anything. I appreciate you for that. I bother you about everything and you put up with me. You were so worried when I was sick. I could see the fear in your eyes. That's the heart of a caring person. You're like a brother to Daniel and he doesn't deserve you."

"Ms. Jamie, please don't say that. Daniel has been good to me. He's like family," Mylow says quietly.

"I know, Mylow. It's so unfair how you've had to be responsible for me the whole time I've lived here. I'm not your responsibility. I came here to be in a relationship with him. I can't hide my feelings anymore. I'm alone and I need something that money nor can this house give me. I need to go to church next Sunday, if you could please take me. I have to go before it's too late. I'm not myself. I feel bad things inside of me and I know this isn't who I am."

"I know you've been through a lot, Ms. Jamie. You hold it all in and that can't be good for you. If you need to go to church, I'll take you."

"Thank you, Mylow. I appreciate you so much."

"Which church would you like to go to?"

"It's a little ways from here. I know I can't go near Mama's house, so I'll go across town."

"Daniel will be back soon. Ms. Jamie, ease up on him, He's going through a lot right now. His patience is really short. I don't know how else to say it, but let him be, at least for a while.

"I'll try," I say, thinking that at this point what can he do but kill me? At least then my living nightmare would finally be over. I haven't had much sleep lately regardless of how much time I've spent in bed. Maybe going to church will help with that.

Loneliness Within

∞∞∞∞

I woke up this morning with a smile on my face. Mylow's taking me to church and I'm so happy about it. This morning I opened all the drapes to let the sunshine in. Something is going to change around here. I don't know what, but I can feel it. I get dressed and head downstairs.

"Mylow? I'm ready," I call out. Mylow steps out of the mudroom.

"The car is ready. You can go out if you want, Ms. Jamie. I'll be out after I lock up." I nod and head out to the car to wait.

As we coast down the highway, I say, "I want to thank you for bringing me to church. I know you're doing this just for me."

"I hope this helps you. I'll do whatever I can do to keep helping Ms. Jamie." He smiles and then looks over at me. "I bet you were a firecracker when you were younger."

I laugh. "Me? No, there was no need to be I was a daddy's girl."

"I can see that," he says thoughtfully.

"One thing I remember most of all was always feeling safe in our home when my dad was alive. We have a back porch and when I was bored, which was usually before he made it home, I would go out there and sit on the edge. I'd dangle my legs off the side and write in my

224

raggedy notebook. I would sit long enough to listen to the birds chirp and write whatever I felt at the time. I'd let myself ramble until all my adolescent worries and thoughts were written down."

"You should try going out on the patio out back," he suggests.

"I could, but it's not the same. Things are different here. No matter what I do, I'll never truly fit in that house or into Daniel's life." I shrug and Mylow looks uncomfortable. "Sorry, I'm rambling."

Mylow doesn't understand that I know Daniel is into bad things. This life he built was done with blood money. But, I shut my mouth, hold it in and go on entertaining Mylow, hoping he relaxes before we get to church. "Oh, we made it right on time. Turn in here, please."

Mylow follows my directions and drives slowly through the packed front parking lot. He looks around warily. "There's more parking in the back," I say.

"There's a lot of folks in church today," he comments. He finds a spot, gets out of the car, and helps me out on my side.

As we approach the church doors, I comment, "Mylow, we can sit in the back. I don't need to be up front."

225

"I'm fine with that," he says. "I haven't been in a church in so many years. I hope I'm not sweating too much right now."

I laugh. "No, you're fine." They must be having some type of church celebration, or something. It's so much busier than it used to be. I see the choir is looking heavenly. I'm glad we came here. This is where I need to be. I feel at peace and so very free right now, at this very moment. I sighed happily, breathing deeply for what felt like the first time in years.

The service was astounding. I cried and cried. The pastor's message was about letting go of pains and things that keep you bound to sin. He said, "Sin gives birth to death. It dryeth the bones." I'm dying on the inside. For one, I'm living in total sin. I've strayed so far from God that I haven't been able to bring myself to pray.

I didn't know if he'd be here, but he was. Jace looked very well today. He addressed the congregation like the man of God he is and asked for volunteers. He spotted me out in the back when he was speaking. He smiled, looking confused. I quickly shook my head before Mylow noticed him looking at me. I can't believe he still has to beg people to help with community outreach. I wish I could help, Lord knows I would. I understand now that we all have a purpose, as Jace would say. I wanted to thank him for helping Mama, but there was no way I could get away from Mylow to do that.

Loneliness Within

The pastor said one other thing that stuck with me throughout the day, "We must allow God in so he can clean out our dirty spaces. We should trust him and cast our cares on him." I think that's beautiful and exactly what I needed.

The song the choir sang was "Hold Me Now." I remember the words so clearly, like they're being sung inside of my head: "Don't you worry God is faithful and He cares. About the tears, you drop and pain you feel He's there. When you are weak, that's when He's strong even though you don't know how. God can and he will hold you now." *Oh God, You hear my voice—You know me by name. You care when no one else does. Deliver me from this madness!* I pray and plead, *Please save me from the loneliness of my pain.*

∞∞∞

I've started writing again. I have a new journal. This is me—Jamie Moore. I'm not what anyone else wants me to be. I can only be me from now on. The life I'm living, everything this man promised me, it was all too good to be true and I should have seen that from the start. Instead, I felt privileged and special. I felt like I needed to be rescued and loved. Those were the lies I told myself. It wasn't really about Steve, or about me wanting to get out of that house. I could have easily moved to campus like I had planned, but I was selfish. I wanted to go off and live this amazing dream life, like Kelsie did. I wanted to show

Mama and Steve I was grown and could live on my own. I understand my selfishness now.

The Bible Daddy bought me I found it the other day. I brought it with me when I moved here, but I never really thought about it until the other day. Funny thing is, it was right in my sight this entire time. But, it wasn't until now that I actually paid attention to it. Now, I'm praying all the time. I'm starting to think maybe I'm not so bad. Maybe I'm not the cause of my baby's death. It just happened, as miscarriages sometimes do. I don't feel so alone inside as much anymore. I have God with me, always.

∞∞∞

Summer 1995

Ms. Janice has stopped coming to clean. She quit, I think. She said her son was really sick and she needed to be closer to home to look after him. I hope her son isn't sick. I think she just had enough of Daniel telling her who she could and couldn't talk to and how to do her job. She was very nice, but she knew more than she let on. I think she found out some things about him too. She just couldn't handle it and found the best, most convenient excuse. I hope nothing bad happens to her if he finds out. We don't have a cleaning lady right now because Daniel can't trust anyone else to come in without him fully investigating who they are. I clean as much as I can and Mylow helps. It's a bit overwhelming though. I have no idea how we make such a mess.

Time moves on and I miss Mama and Kelsie so much. I pray for them all the time. I've forgiven myself for my feelings about the miscarriage. I never had the courage to ask the doctors what really happened, but I know the truth. I'm okay with all of it now. Daniel doesn't talk to me and he doesn't try to sleep near me anymore either. He looks worried though, more now than ever. He's aging fast. I guess the lies and evil are taking a toll on him. He's on edge and very angry most of the time. I'm afraid of him, so I stay completely out of his way.

I sure hope Ms. Janice mailed Mama the letters I wrote her. She could have read them and gotten scared, deciding she wanted to get away from this place. All I can do now is wait and hope that Jace seeing me will get him to talk to her. We can't keep going on this way. If I never make it out of here alive, I want to be happy until that day comes. I believe there's more to life for me though. I'll keep praying and believing someone will find out what's going on. Then, I can finally be free.

It's been nearly four weeks and we finally have a new cleaning lady. She's very different from Ms. Janice. She's around my age and she wears very tight and revealing cleaning outfits. I think she has her eye on Mylow. She wants him to look at her so bad. It's kind of obvious and pathetic, definitely desperate. She's cute, though. I wonder what her story is and how it will unfold. She doesn't speak English very well, which makes it hard to communicate with her. Mr. Daniel chose her personally, so she might be for him—who knows?

I've been in this house for a few years. I've seen things that I had to ignore, knowing they were wrong. I know Daniel meets up with different women when he's at the condo. He has a dark side of him and he tries to mask it from me. He has a monster inside him, but he tries to put it in the closet when I'm around. His eyes can't lie. I can see the guilt bleeding out of them. The more I pray, the more I see things clearly. Daniel's on his way back home today. Mylow was up and at it early this morning. I'm glad I'm not so worried about spending time with him anymore.

A few hours after Daniel returned, he asked me—completely out of the blue—if he could sleep in bed with me tonight. He had a strange expression too. I have no idea what it meant. It's something I've never seen before. It kind of reminded of a child looking to their mom for approval. He also said some things I can't seem to shake from my thoughts. He acknowledged being completely absent from me while I've been here. Then, he went on to say he understood why I didn't want a child and that the world is cruel and unpredictable, which he said was a big enough reason not to want a child. He's never talked to me like this before. I agreed he could sleep with me tonight. I didn't want to turn him down after such an honest confession and I think I can handle one night. He said he didn't want to be alone, but the really interesting part about this is that it's the first time he's ever asked me to do anything.

Who is this person?

Later that night, as Daniel climbs into bed with me, I can't keep my thoughts in my head.

I set down my book and turn to him. "How is it that all this time—since I've been with you—all of a sudden you want to acknowledge my pain and try to understand me? Why now when it's just too late?"

Daniel takes a moment to think about his response, which is far nicer than I thought I would get after asking that question.

"Jamie, I would be angry if I were you too."

"I thought you were so different when I met you. You aren't at all who I thought you were, Daniel."

"But you are, Jamie. You're soft, gentle, and attentive."

I can't take the flattery, not when I think he's being insincere, or at least out to get something. "No, I was nothing more than a piece to your puzzle. I was a ploy for you to gain clout with certain people, so you could do business with them. You wanted to fit in. I was a small moving piece to this game called life you created."

"No, I needed you to help me see reality. You made me feel again, but it scared me. I was too deep in my world to change. I was someone you didn't know and I was ruining you. I felt badly every time I looked into your eyes,

I still do. I should have never brought you here. You deserved so much more than this."

The more he talks, the more he apologizes, the angrier I become. "Why now, Daniel? Why say this to me now? Is there something going on?"

"Yes, there's always something going on. I'm tired of fighting. No matter what happens, Jamie, I want you to know I have loved you since the first day I saw you. I've had an insane way of showing you. I didn't even tell you until you were pregnant, I know, but I always felt it. I'm a bad person who has done really bad things in his life. I'm sorry. There are so many things I want to say to you."

Daniel burrows under the covers and rests his head in my lap. I gently rub my palm over the crown of his head, unsure what to do. This is so strange. I don't think we've ever sat like this before.

"Tell me where this is coming from? You're scaring me right now," I murmur.

"You always put me first—like now, even before yourself and your own feelings."

"I did it because I loved you," I say, crying. "I've loved you since that first day I ran into you and made you drop your stuff. You shut me out for so long. I've been afraid of you, afraid of disappointing you. I've spent so much time stuck in this house and feeling so alone. I lost sight of who I was."

Daniel nods sadly. "Jamie, you deserve more than this screwed up world of mine."

Tears quietly track down his face. "Please don't do this," I say. "You can't fix it now. I'm mad at myself because somewhere deep inside I still love you, even after all of this. I have longed to be held by you, touched by you, and loved by you for so long."

"Jamie, I need serious help. You'll never understand," Daniel says. I move to kiss his cheek, but he intercepts me and the kiss becomes passionate. I let him take control of it.

After we make love, he falls asleep quickly. I lie awake, hating myself. Why did I do that? God forgive me! How could I make love to that man, that monster? I'm so disappointed in myself. It's too late for this right now. He's holding me so tightly. It feels secure and safe, but I know he's not a safe man. I wonder what brought all of this on. What has he done?

∞∞∞∞

This must be a nightmare…I can't believe I'm sitting outside in a police car! I'm shaking—maybe I'm in shock. Everything happened so fast. There was a loud bang then gunshots in the house. I sat up in the bed and tried to wake Daniel, but he wouldn't wake up. Before I could get up to see what was going on, the police busted in, flooding the bedroom and forcing us to the ground.

Daniel didn't put up a fight. They asked him to state his name and he refused to say a word. They arrested him. The officer said he was being arrested for conspiracy to commit murder, manslaughter, kidnapping, and illegal wire transfers. They took him out of the house immediately and settled him into a squad car. I sat there in disbelief. Relief flooding my system, but I was so scared. I didn't want the police to think I had anything to do with his business.

Just when I started to pray, I heard a familiar voice call me. She helped me off the floor. It was Ms. Janice! But not the Ms. Janice I once knew. It was a new and improved younger lady with a gun and a badge and no accent.

"Ms. Janice? What are you doing here?"

"Jamie, my name isn't Janice. I'm Special Agent Charlene Roma." I stare, shocked, as she continued, "I was sent in undercover two years before you moved in. I hadn't intended to be there that long, but I wanted to help you."

"You didn't need to do that."

Agent Roma chuckles. "I wanted to blow my cover to tell you to get out and go as far away as I could, but I couldn't risk all the work I'd put into building a solid case against Daniel and the others involved." I nodded.

"I'm sorry," I say, for lack of anything better.

She shushes me and says that I was the reason she fought to bring him down sooner rather than later. She couldn't accept me being a part of Daniel's life knowing the things he had done. She said she'd never met a more honest and caring person in her life. She told me I had a bright future waiting for me and not to let what happened tonight or any other time I was here affect who I was meant to be.

Agent Roma looks me square in the eye and says, "Thank you for giving me purpose again. Thank you for reminding me of what my real responsibilities were."

Those letters I wrote Mama never reached her. There was too much evidence in those letters for Mama to have possession of them. They didn't want her trying to find me and putting herself in danger. They had to handle this case on a federal level. Not very many people could be trusted, especially not anyone local who could be tied to them.

Soon after Ms. Janice left the house, Agent Roma arranged for someone to visit Mama and explain the situation. So, she was told that I was okay. I'm happy about that at least.

"What happened with the gunshots I heard in the house?" I ask Agent Roma.

"Mylow was wounded, but he's okay. He was taken to the hospital. Once he's released, he'll be immediately detained." I nod, not trusting myself to speak anymore. I'm too tired from all of this mess.

An officer approaches. "Excuse me, Agent Roma. We need to take her to the station and get an official statement from her." My eyes dart to Agent Roma, scared.

She smiles at me. "Oh, don't worry honey. It's just protocol. You could go in the morning if you'd like?"

I shake my head. I'd rather get it over with. "I don't have a car," I mutter.

The officer smiles. "Ever been in the back of a patrol car?" I shake my head. "Come on, my partner and I will take you. Then, we'll arrange for someone to get you home, okay?"

I nod and follow the officer to the car. As we drive, the officers tell me they'll ask questions about what I know, if anything, about Daniel's business dealings. They'll want to know anything I remember because even small details might help the case. I struggle to think about what I might know.

We pull into the station and everything goes exactly as they say. A nice officer gets me a cup of coffee and a pastry. We sit down in an interrogation room, so the conversation can be recorded, and I give my statement. Once it's done, they say I'll be free to go, but we've been at this for hours. I haven't really stopped crying since this all started. My eyes are so tired it feels like they're filled with sand.

Daniel must have known this was going to happen. That's what all the conversation was about last night. I pray for him to find his way to God. Anyone can change with God's help, if they want to. Mylow, oh God, I hope he's all right. He will have to do his time too for the part he played in all of this. Agent Roma said he was a lot more involved than I realized. I don't care anymore. I'm just thrilled that my nightmare is over!

They asked me about the photo IDs. I told them I didn't know anything about them, but that I saw them in the office, hidden in a book. They said those were people on the IDs were kidnapped by Daniel and his business partners. They tried to get away with large amounts of money they borrowed from people Daniel worked with, and he was the one who made sure they paid up or disappeared. The cops know most of them from being in and out of jail. With the IDs, they can easily look them up in the system, at least. Almost each and every one of them had their own share of petty crimes, if not worse.

I struggle to clear my throat. "Detective," I ask the cop questioning me, "who was dead man in the picture?"

"Ah, that was a friend of Daniel's. He's not actually dead. They had him made up in makeup—like in the movies—to convince some very powerful people he'd been killed, so he could get out of the debt he owed them. Now, some of the others from the IDs are unaccounted for, so we have to assume they're dead, but for the most part, everyone you saw is alive and more or less well." I breathed a sigh of relief. Maybe now I could get the "dead" man's eyes out of my mind.

"Don't worry," the detective says, "This is the beginning of a series of arrests. Daniel and his friends have been under investigation for a long time and they have a lot coming to them." Grateful, I nod and we continue with the statement and questioning.

By the time I've told these people everything I remember, it's been over five hours of sitting here. We went through week-by-week, month-by-month, in as much detail as I could recall. I'm so tired. I want to go home. They brought me my purse and my Bible like I asked. That's all that matters to me from that place. They can have all of that stuff. I don't want any of it. It was paid for with blood money and I have no need for it.

"Ms. Moore, you're free to go," the detective says. "We'll be in touch if we need more information or have additional questions. I believe your family is waiting outside for you."

"Thank you, sir!" I say as I rush out of the claustrophobic room. I see Mama waiting off to the side and I run to her. "Mama! Oh Mama!" I yell, pulling her close and burying my face in her hair. "I can't believe this is over. I missed you so much!" I gently pull away and look around. I'm shocked to see another familiar face. "Jace! You're here! Thank you so much for all you've done for my family. I'll never be able to repay you," I say as I pull him into a hug too.

"I would do it all over again, Jamie," he says thoughtfully.

"Let's get out of here. Oh God, I'm going home. I can't wait to go home."

"Not just home, baby, but a newly renovated home," Mama says, smiling at Jace.

Jace and Mama lead me out to his car. We climb inside and settle in. Mama speaks as soon as we're on our way, "A lot has changed since you left, Jamie."

"So I've heard."

"What did you hear?" she asks, confused.

"Never mind, Mama. So, you have a new home?"

"Yes, thanks to this man right here."

"I can't wait to see it. How does Mr. Steve like it?"

"Who?" Mama asks, laughing.

"Steve. Mama, come on. You know who I'm talking about," I say, too tired to be patient with her joking.

"Oh, that man's been gone a long while. I put him out after you left. Kelsie told me everything. She was so upset with me."

I'm stunned. It was that easy? Why couldn't she have seen it when Steve and I were fighting? I mean, I know I didn't tell her, but she knew about the tension between us.

"Why didn't you tell me, Jamie?"

239

Loneliness Within

I shrug and look out the window. "We'll talk about it later, but right now—oh Mama!" We pull up to a grand old house that sits right where our other house used to be. "This can't be our old house," I say as I take in the paint, new door, and windows. There's even a new roof.

"Yes, it is!"

"Oh, Jace, how did you get this done?" I ask as we all head inside. It's just as gorgeous inside as it is out.

"It's a long story," he says, grinning. "Maybe we'll get a chance to talk about it once you've had a chance to get settled."

"Jamie, honey, God has been so good to me. He brought you out of that mess alive and well. I couldn't be more thankful."

Jace clears his throat lightly. "I better go. Ya'll have a lot to catch up on. It was good to see you, Jamie."

"Jace, let me walk you back to the car, please."

"You don't have to, Ms. Jamie."

"No, I want to," I say. Jace nods. Mama heads inside and I follow him back to his car.

"Thank you so much for being there for Mama. I want you to know that coming to the church that Sunday saved my life. I thought I was going to die. I was in a very dark place, but in that service, at that moment, I learned who God was to me. Not to you or my daddy or anyone else—just who God was in my life. I learned what He means to me. And seeing you speak with such purpose and direction showed me that I couldn't let myself die in my situation. I didn't know when or how I'd get out of that mess, but I felt like I would somehow. I could feel it in my bones. After that, I began to pray and talk to God myself. I read my Bible and I remembered scriptures from when I was younger. They came back to me, some of them. I'm not the same person I was when I left here. In more than one way, I've changed." I stand there awkwardly for a moment as he thinks about what I've just said. "Anyway, thank you for your prayers and thank you for helping Mama get a new house when I couldn't. I owe you so much!"

Finally, he speaks up again, "See, that's the thing, Jamie. You don't owe me anything. It was all God's doing."

At that, I burst into tears again. "If I could just stop crying!" I sniffed.

"No, don't. You have the right to cry." He steps close and pulls me into a tight hug. "You are the strongest woman I've ever met and I'm so blessed to know you."

I step away from him and wipe my face. "You are too kind. I should go inside. I think I need to rest."

"Whatever I can do, I will, just let me know," he says.

"No Jace! You've done more than enough. I'll talk with you later, but thank you for your kind offer."

"I'll be back to check on you tomorrow."

"Okay," I say as I turn and head back into the house. I can hear his car start up behind me. "Mama," I call out, shutting the door behind me. "I still can't believe how amazing this house looks. It's brand new—even the furniture is new."

"You should get some rest, Jamie. You look awfully tired."

"I am," I sigh.

"I have your bed freshly made, it's all yours again." I smile softly. Mama purses her lips and touches my arm. "I want to say again that I'm so sorry about Steve and how he treated you girls. I don't think I really understood what it was like for you. I thought you just didn't get along." Mama pauses and I wait, letting her continue at her own pace. "I'm also very sorry for not being here for you mentally or emotionally. I've blamed myself for you leaving and for you feeling like you had to go live in that hell. I've spent many nights asking God to save you and asking him for forgiveness."

I nod in understanding and I try to say something, but she cuts me off before I can get a word out.

"I'm different, Jamie. I'm stronger than I've ever been before. I should have been your mother, not your responsibility. I love you, baby, and I've been waiting to tell you that." I wrap my arms around my mother, holding her close.

"Mama, don't do this. I can't cry another tear. My eyes are so tired of crying. I know you love me. You were going through so much at that time. I understand and I forgive you."

She nods happily, tears sliding down her face too. What's so amazing is to see my mama back to herself and not seeing Steve walk around here being mean and hateful.

"Mama that man was just nasty!" Mama laughs and I smile. "Okay, I got it out. I can move on now." We both laugh and then settle into the quiet for a moment. "We'll talk later, okay, Mama?" She nods and I head to my room.

∞∞∞∞

The next morning, I wake up slowly. After I get myself together, I knock on Mama's door quietly, not wanting to wake her if she isn't already up.

"Mama, are you up?" I ask, gently knocking again.

"Yes, come in," she says through the door. She's up and making her bed with her nightgown still on.

"How's Kelsie doing?" I ask, settling next to Mama on the bed.

243

"Oh baby, you don't know do you?"

"Know what?" I ask, suddenly worried. Did Kelsie get hurt?

"Your sister is pregnant and getting married in a couple of months. She's sending for me. We were praying you would be home before then. She wanted you there with her." Mama gives me that look. "You should call her. She needs you. This is a scary time for her. Now that you're home, you can be there to celebrate her becoming a mother and wife."

"A baby? Kelsie's a mama?"

"Yes, we would prefer marriage first, but it's too late for that. She's happy with a wonderful man. I haven't met him in person, but I've had quite few conversations with him over the phone. He seems like a nice, good man."

"What about her father?" I can't help but ask.

"Well, it was strange at first, but more for her than Ben. He was so happy to see her," she says. "He told her she brought back some of his best childhood memories and failures. He wanted to know everything about her. I think he must have asked a lot about me."

"Why?" I ask, puzzled.

"He knew too much about me when we spoke over the phone and you know Kelsie, she isn't the one to go sharing personal information without being prompted."

"I bet you're right."

"He's still as handsome as ever, Kelsie said. And very caring towards others. He took her around right away to meet his other kids from his ex-wife."

"Ex-wife?" I can sense a whole bunch of trouble coming if that's why she's going.

"Yes, he told me they divorced a few years ago. He never felt like she really loved him, just the lifestyle they lived. They shared custody of the youngest child, but now all of them are grown."

"Really? I see you've talked to him quite a bit, Mama."

"We've talked a few times, but it was mostly about Kelsie," Mama insists.

"Are you sure?" I ask warily.

"Yes! It's not like that, Jamie Annette Moore! We're cordial and polite. He's always been a great person to talk to, we're friends."

"I guess I've missed so much these past couple of years."

"You'll get to see him at the wedding."

"Yes, but this trip to California is about Kelsie."

"I agree, nothing more. What Ben and I had years ago is over now. We're both in very different places in our lives and having old feelings come up is the furthest thing from my mind."

I nod, grateful that she isn't going to try to win him back. But Mama being with a man she once loved so much might not be so bad. I'm not so naive to think she wouldn't want to be loved by a man like Mr. Ben.

"So, California worked out after all for my big sis."

"Yes, she works with her father at the clinic. She's still in school. She found her calling, Jamie. She knows what she wants in life for once." Mama pauses. "I'd like to be there when the baby comes. I haven't told her yet, but I'm going back to California around her due date. I want to help her with the baby. I think the change would be good for me. You should come too," she urges. "Maybe getting out of Texas for a while will do you some good."

"No, I feel like I just got back. It feels almost like I've been far away and trying to find my way home. Kind of like Dorothy in the Wizard of Oz." Mama frowns. "I don't know, Mama. I need to figure out my next move in life."

Mama nods understandingly. "Just take it one day at a time."

Chapter Fourteen

Fall 1995

I slam the door behind me as I stomp out onto the porch, a regular ball of fury these days.

"Jace! Why do you keep coming here? What's your agenda? What do you want from me? I have nothing to give." He opens his mouth, but I don't let him speak. "Listen to me, please! I'm dry. I'm emotionally bankrupt! I look in your eyes, not to see the good, but to search for your hidden secrets—everyone has them. I'm waiting for you to disconnect, just like everyone else has in the past. Is that fair to you? No, of course not, but it's the truth." I sigh heavily as I lose my anger. "Look Jace, I know you're good man, but another part of me thinks my judgment of men is screwed up. I can't trust right now."

"Ms. Jamie Annette Moore, you listen to me! I have loved you for as long as I have known you. You're special, one of a kind. I admire you. I know you've been in a bad place, but I'm tired of hiding my feelings for you. I'll wait if I have to. I'll be patient, but hear me out! Don't keep me outside too long. I'm not asking for your hand in marriage. All I want is dinner, a movie, a walk in the park, and maybe a laugh or two from you. Is that too much to ask for? Now, I know you need space and time; I get that. But I would like to help you move on."

I can't bear to hear him. Why is he still so concerned with me?

"Jace, why do you love someone like me? I'm still a little broken and damaged inside. I'm not fit for dating."

"You're everything I want in a woman. You're strong. You're smart. You love first and ask questions later, which is a rare quality." I scoff.

"Look how well that worked out for me."

He ignores me and continues, "You have so much inside, Jamie. I love you because I can't help it. When you were gone, I tried not to and failed. The poem you wrote for me told me of your true heart's condition. But, it's cold out here, outside these stone walls of yours. I want to see more of your smile. Can you at least allow me to take you to a movie?"

I sigh heavily. "Yes, but let me call you okay?"

"Okay, that's a start. I'll be waiting."

Jace takes off and I head back inside. Mama approaches me, frowning.

"Jamie, why are you doing that man like that? He's a good man. He's honest and loving. Look at all he's done for you and for me! What has happened to you?" she asks, concern in her voice. I can't take it anymore.

"Mama, life happened! I'm not the same person I was. For the last couple of years, I've been locked away in a house alone, mostly scared, and trying to love a man who only loved himself. I felt so neglected and alone, even when he was in bed with me. I lived with the devil and I thought I loved him, despite knowing he was capable of anything. I hated myself, Mama!"

"I know, Jamie, but you have to put this behind you, once and for all. You have to change the way you think about your life. In some ways, you're still stuck there, but it's in your mind.

"You have to transform your thinking. I had to learn that lesson for myself, baby. I was still mourning old situations and things that happened to me. I didn't really know my daddy because I was too young to remember him clearly. My relationship with my Mama? Lord knows that was bad. I had to share her with the folks she worked for and their children. Sometimes, she'd treat them better than she did me. I made one mistake and she disowned me. The neglect from that was devastating.

"Then, she died and I couldn't fix it. I should have been there to help her, but I was too bitter. When your daddy died, baby, I felt like God hated me. I didn't want to go on. So, I know what pain, suffering, and loneliness feel like. I decided I wanted something different for my future. I didn't want to be stuck anymore. I changed my mind about the way I thought about my past—that's how I broke free. You have to lean on God, Jamie, and decide you're no longer the young, scared woman who lived in that house." Mama's words were difficult to hear, but they rung true.

"Mama, every day is a little bit better, but I don't think Jace understands what I'm dealing with."

"He does. He thinks he can love you out of it, but he can't. Be patient and talk to him, but try to leave your anger behind."

I nod. It's not Jace's fault and I shouldn't take it out on him. "I will," I say. "I'm sorry. You're right. I need to change the way I chose to feel on the inside. I can't go back and change the past, but I can do something about right now. I love you, Mama. I guess I'll call him later."

Mama nods and starts to head back to the kitchen, but I catch her arm. She turns back.

"Kelsie and I talked for over two hours this morning." Mama smiles, bright as sunshine. "She asked me to come to California for a few months. She thinks I need to get away from here. I said I could tell you two have been talking too. She told me that I'd love the ocean and that there's so much to do. She thought maybe I could take a look at the college and talk to them about transferring, if that was something I wanted to do."

Mama nodded. "What else is in that head of yours, baby?"

"I've been thinking real hard, and when we leave next week, I don't think I'm coming back. I will one day, but I think I'll stay there for a while."

"Oh, that's great, Jamie!" I didn't expect Mama to be so happy about my leaving. She was devastated last time. I guess we both have grown. "What about Jace? Do you plan on telling him that you're headed to your sister's for a couple of months?"

"Yes, I am. I'm sure he'll want what's best for me. In fact, I'll invite him to the movies tonight and I'll tell him then. I know it's not the best timing, but I don't know what else to do."

"You're going to break his heart," Mama says, frowning.

"I don't mean to, but I'm not ready to be in a relationship. I need a fresh start. I have to start somewhere so why not now?"

"That's my girl," Mama says. "I'm so proud of you. You're much stronger than I ever was."

When Jace and I went to the movies, I told him about my plans and he was happy for me. He thought getting away from here would do me some good and he said he'd been talking to God about some things and this was confirmation. I'm not sure what that means, but it

251

didn't sound bad. He asked me to send him pictures and a postcard. I said I'd send him something every month.

I know God is reminding me of what love should look like through Jace. I almost forgot all the wonderful things my daddy would say and do for Mama. I told Jace that no matter what we'll be friends forever. I hope he can get away and come visit Kelsie and me in California. He said he would definitely try to come visit. We'll see.

Chapter Fifteen

We arrived in California late last night. Kelsie's home is so cute and so is her fiancé. He's awful nice and no one said he was white. It's funny that she failed to tell us that little fact. But, the apple doesn't fall far from the tree, I suppose. I guess she wanted us to see him not by his color, but by the way he treated her. I'm amazed at how good they are together. He moved in with his parents for a few days since he knew we were coming. He wanted to give her time with us alone. And since she found out she was pregnant they've been celibate. She told us they've been finding it difficult to maintain that commitment. Oh, Kelsie—she has a wicked sense of humor. I told her it was a little too late for celibacy and she laughed too. But I've learned everyone will do what they want their own way. She told me I was as beautiful as ever, but she's the one glowing with love and happiness. We hugged, talked, and laughed for a while.

Tonight, Mama's going to dinner with Mr. Ben. They say it's just dinner. He had asked her out before we even got here, but who knows? They might fall back in love after all these years. She deserves to be happy. She's suffered long enough—we all have. Kelsie and I are taking her to get a makeover before their date. We want her to have a new look for her new self.

Mama loves us both and we know it. I know she wants to ask Mr. Ben a lot of questions, questions that have been sitting for a long, long time. She wants to put their past to rest. She suppressed it for so long.

∞∞∞

After the makeover, Kels and I brought out a surprise we'd gone in on together for Mama, just to make her night a little more special.

"Mama," I say after we get home from the salon, "I know we forced you to go through that intense makeover, but we have one more thing for you."

"What is it now?" she asks.

Kelsie smiles. "No pressure, but we have a special outfit for you to wear tonight!" We hold out the box and watch her open it. Her eyes light up as she touches the vibrant blue material of the dress.

"Thank you, girls, but y'all didn't have to do that."

"We know, Mama, but we wanted to," I say. "Before it gets too late, Mama, I want to talk to you and Kelsie." Concern crosses their faces.

"Okay, we're here," Kelsie says.

"While I was with Daniel, I got pregnant." I hold my breath as I wait for their reactions.

"What?" Mama asks. Kelsie's hand goes to cover her lower belly.

I took a deep breath. "Daniel wanted a baby so badly. He thought it would make him good and maybe make his life worth living again. I wasn't pregnant long, but during the pregnancy, I was very sick. I couldn't stop throwing up. I was so dehydrated that it almost killed me. I was about two months along. I had to be hospitalized and the baby didn't survive. I miscarried."

"Oh, Jamie, I'm so sorry," Kelsie says with tears in her eyes.

"Wait, let me get this out before you guys get all emotional on me. I never wanted the baby. I prayed and prayed God would take it from me. I hated Daniel at the time, and I knew he was doing some really bad things. I didn't want to bring a baby into a situation like that. For the longest time, I believed I willed my baby to die.

"I began to hate myself for it. But with God's help, prayer, and understanding, I know that I had no power to create or end life. It was up to God. That power belongs to Him. So, I'm free of that guilt and shame. It took me a long time to realize it, but I know the doctors tried everything, but because of the prolonged dehydration and weakness, the baby couldn't thrive. Kelsie, it wasn't until I found out you're pregnant that those feelings came back to me.

"One day, I'll get married and have children of my own, but I'm not ready for that right now. I'm so happy at this very moment. I have my best friend here who's about to get married and have a baby of her own. And Mama, my rock, but most importantly, I have God. He lives in my heart.

"This is a beautiful day and I am so thankful for it. The dark mornings have come and gone. I don't have anything to complain about, not one thing. I want to share something I wrote a few weeks ago. It's called *Morning Glory*."

GOD be close to my heart,
So immensely glorified each day from the start.
Let the morning sunrise reminisce of your everlasting love.
May the world look through me and see purity like a dove:
evidence of you.
Expressions surrounding this enormous land called earth.
Come home peace, rest in my soul.
Welcome back joy;
Pour out a fresh new praise powerful and bold.
Shut down the strong holds,
Uncover the secrets and treasures
On earth as it is in heaven.
Rise glory Rise;
Show your divine favor.
Shine light shine;
Releasing sprinkles of your sweet, sweet savior.

Loneliness Within

Rest Upon Me.

I read the poem aloud to my mother and sister.

"Jamie, that was amazing," Kelsie says, wiping tears from her eyes.

"Thanks, Kels. Now, look at you, Mama. Your makeup is all messed up now!" Kelsie laughs and I smile.

"Oh my! What am I going to do now? It's getting late!"

"Don't worry, Mama," Kelsie says, just as I say, "Kels will fix it, Mama." Kelsie and I laugh at each other.

"Go into the bathroom and get dressed, we'll do your makeup afterword," Kelsie says.

"Okay, I love you both." Mama walks away with a smile on her face.

"We love you too," I call out.

Kelsie watches Mama go, but then turns to me. "Jamie, you are a strong woman. I'm so proud to be your sister. I know we've been through so much, but now we can be happy. I mean, look at us now! Look how far we've come!"

∞∞∞∞

I've been in California for nearly six months now and I'm helping Kelsie a lot with the baby. I'm also in school for nursing. I work with Mr. Ben at the clinic for now. Once I'm done with school, he has friends at the hospital who will connect me with my first nursing job. I couldn't be more excited.

Thankfully, I didn't have to testify against Daniel. There was so much evidence against him and they didn't need me—I didn't know much anyway. Apparently, soon after his arrest Daniel had a bit of a breakdown and needed psychiatric help. I pray for him all the time. Mylow wasn't charged with as much. He'll see freedom one day and hopefully start over.

My life is so different now. I find myself smiling just because. I love to walk near the ocean. I drive down and sit out on the sand, looking out into the never-ending sky and praying. I talk to Jace all the time. He's been here once to visit. He fell in love with California just like I did. We spent the entire time sightseeing and talking. He's decided to move here.

He's going on a mission trip to Africa in a month, and when he returns to the States, he's moving out here. He wants to go to college and live near the school. His brother and parents are paying for him get his degree. He always said God has a purpose for each of us. He knew he was only passing through on his journey of life. He did what he was appointed to do and now it's time for him to move on. The church wished him well and decided they would donate three months of rent to pay for his place here. Now that is God working things out, he hasn't decided what he wants to take up yet.

As for me, I'm taking my time enjoying life. If I truly trust and love God like I say I do, how can I ever feel loneliness within like I did so often before?

I can't. I won't. I refuse. It's impossible. God is always with me.

Acknowledgements

To my amazing children, *Dasia* and *Devin* I love you, to my mother *Karen* that always believed in my vision, my siblings whom I love dearly and my aunt *Doris*.

I have been under the great ministry of Bishop T.D. Jakes for 19 years. Over the years I have learned to think differently, dream bigger, believe more in my God given purpose to journey forward through this remarkable life.

Thank you, Kevin Anderson, & Associates for all of your hard work and to the team at Signarama (Frisco) for the amazing cover design. Also, I want to give a heartfelt thanks to the countless people that poured out their support throughout this life-changing journey.

GOD the Father is the reason I am here at this magnificent point in my life. I can now help others along the way. Thank you Master for choosing a sinner like me!

About the Author…

L. Diane Estes is a native of the great state of Texas. Early in her studies she received a degree in Psychology. When she is not traveling, she ghost writes for new authors. She also enjoys writing poetry and short stories. With a family of educators, she was inclined to follow the legacy and later pursued her Master's in Higher Education with a Communications specification. Diane is very passionate about the power of communication and provoking others to find their inner creative expression through diverse literary art forms.

www.ldianeestes.com